Ann Cleeves

Ann Cleeves is the author behind ITV's VERA and BBC One's SHETLAND. She has written over twenty-five novels, and is the creator of detectives Vera Stanhope and Jimmy Perez – characters loved both on screen and in print. Her books have now sold over one million copies worldwide.

Ann worked as a probation officer, bird observatory cook and auxiliary coastguard before she started writing. She is a member of 'Murder Squad', working with other British northern writers to promote crime fiction. In 2006 Ann was awarded the Duncan Lawrie Dagger (CWA Gold Dagger) for Best Crime Novel, for *Raven Black*, the first book in her Shetland series. In 2012 she was inducted into the CWA Crime Thriller Awards Hall of Fame. Ann lives in North Tyneside.

Ann Cleeves

A LESSON
IN DYING

BELL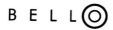

First published in 1990 by Century

This edition published 2014 by Bello
an imprint of Pan Macmillan, a division of Macmillan Publishers Limited
Pan Macmillan, 20 New Wharf Road, London N1 9RR
Basingstoke and Oxford
Associated companies throughout the world

www.panmacmillan.co.uk/bello

ISBN 978-1-4472-5318-1 EPUB
ISBN 978-1-4472-8909-8 POD

A CIP catalogue record for this book is available from the British Library.

*To the pupils and staff of
Holywell First School –
to which Heppleburn Primary
bears no resemblance at all.*

Chapter One

At one time you could see fifteen working mines from Heppleburn churchyard. Now the nearest pit was miles away to the north beyond the horizon and only the chimneys of Blyth power station spoilt the impression of rural beauty. To the east farmland sloped down to the sea, the clean sweep of ploughed fields broken by the wooded valley which followed the burn to the coast and the houses of Heppleburn village. The sea was blue, almost purple, the tower of the old St Mary's Island lighthouse was clear and white in the sunshine. Jack Robson put a bunch of chrysanthemums on his wife's grave. He had come with flowers every week since she had died two years before.

The school and the church stood together on the hill, and as he straightened he heard children singing 'We plough the fields and scatter'. The Northumberland voices shortened the consonants and lightened the vowels. Jack Robson had sung the same hymn in exactly the same way more than fifty years before in Heppleburn school. He thought he had wasted his time there. It seemed to him now that he had been a dull and unimaginative boy. There had been no dreams, no ambition. It had never occurred to him that he might move away from south-east Northumberland, and during National Service he thought of nothing but coming home. People said that the mind grew slower as it got older, but he thought his brain was sharper now than it had ever been. With his retirement from the pit he had begun to read voraciously as some children do, and became immersed especially in history and biography. He found he could understand what he read, that he even occasionally had the courage to disagree with the opinions expressed.

The new confidence was noticed by other people. He had been a habitual member of the local Labour Party for years – his father had been a great activist and it was expected.

More recently he had been asked to stand for the local council, and now as Councillor Robson he represented Heppleburn on Hepple Valley District Council. He was especially respected by his younger colleagues, for his openmindedness and his willingness to accept innovation, but he spoke in meetings of the old morality, the old principles, in a way that stirred them all.

'Why do you bother with the job at the school?' one of the younger men asked, implying, despite his politics, that manual labour was something to be ashamed of.

Robson shrugged. He could have said that he needed the money, which was true enough, but there was more to it than that. He liked the children and feeling part of a team. He was a school governor but he had more contact with the children through his work. Besides, what else could he do?

He looked at his watch and began to walk through the churchyard towards the school. In the distance a tractor was ploughing a newly harvested field with immaculate furrows, followed by a cloud of white gulls. The children had stopped singing. The school bell rang and as he reached the gate the pupils began to run into the playground on their way home. He waited to wave to his grandchildren then went in. He was the school caretaker. It was a job that suited him, despite the headmaster. He knew there would a Parents' Association meeting that evening and began to set out tables and chairs in the hall. Lily, the cleaner, arrived on her bicycle and they shared a joke and a gossip while they worked. At five o'clock he left and walked down the hill to the red-brick council house where he had lived since he was first married.

The Parents' Association meeting took place on the Friday before the Blackberry Week half term. Jack Robson's daughter was there and the Hallowe'en party discussed by the meeting was her idea. Like all her ideas it was formed on the spur of the moment and ill thought through.

'You're mad,' her husband said later that evening when she got home and told him about it.

'I thought you were fed up with the Parents' Association and now you've landed yourself a job like this.'

'It might be fun,' Patty said, still excited because her idea had been agreed by the headmaster, her head still full of plans.

'I'm surprised Medburn agreed.'

'So am I,' she said.

'You only took it on because you're bored,' Jim said. 'You should get a job.'

He was right. With the children both at school she had been restless for months. She had even nagged her husband about moving somewhere a bit more stylish – perhaps to Morpeth or on the coast, but Jim knew she would never leave Heppleburn. Besides, he said, how could they afford to move on a teacher's salary? If she wanted a change she could go back to work. His mother would mind the bairns when they came out of school. Patty recognized the sense of his suggestion but knew she would not be satisfied with working as a clerk at the Gas Board again and realized she was qualified for nothing else. At eighteen she had left home to go to a teacher training college in Reading, but after a fortnight she was ill with homesickness and came home to her mam and dad in Heppleburn. The experience had made her glad then of the job in the accounts office, the security and the company of the other girls. Now she knew she would hate it. If only I had qualifications! she thought, and wondered hopelessly about the Open University, but she realized she would never have the application to complete a degree.

During this period of restlessness she had paid for evening classes and attended a few sessions, but never finished the course. She had taken up aerobics, dressmaking and archery and launched into each new interest with the conviction that it would meet all her needs. The conviction soon passed. She had been for wild nights out to the clubs in Whitley Bay with friends from her old job, but only woke up with a hangover and the same feeling of dissatisfaction. She had considered having a baby, even, in moments of deep depression when the day was empty except for cleaning windows and weeding Jim's beloved garden, she had considered finding a lover, but she knew herself well enough to know that her enthusiasm for these projects would end long before the resulting complications.

'Well,' she said, looking at Jim through the untidy fringe which irritated him so much, 'it'll keep me busy for a few weeks.'

She had conceived the plan for the Hallowe'en party on the way to the meeting. The church and the school were apart from the village, reached by a steep footpath between hawthorn hedges. The haws were forming and the leaves were beginning to change colour. Although she was late Patty stood for a moment in the playground. She came to school every day to bring her children, but she had a sudden memory of her own childhood there, never previously recalled. It was a freezing winter's day, grey and overcast, with flurries of snow, the flakes as small and painful as hail. Her knees and hands had been blue in the bitter wind which came uninterrupted from the North Sea. Miss Hunt had let them into the classroom early and they stood around the big, evil-smelling boiler in the corner until their flesh tingled with the unaccustomed warmth. Miss Hunt had been her first teacher and Patty had loved her passionately. Now she taught Patty's daughter Jennifer and soon she would retire.

The school had been smaller in Patty's day and so had the village. Its heart had been the main street of solid grey houses, with the post office and the Northumberland Arms. There had been the small council estate where her father still lived and she had been brought up, and the row of miners' welfare cottages where old men coughed and spluttered and smoked themselves to death. The children had fitted easily into two classrooms – the infants in one and the juniors in another. In recent years the village had grown. Builders had bought the low land near the burn and turned it into the estate where she and Jim lived. It was similar to other estates surrounding other villages all over the country. Most of the homes now had swings in the back garden and a bike in the garage and the school had expanded into a series of mobile and new classrooms.

I was happy in this school, Patty thought, longing for the contentment of childhood. But she knew that even then she had been unruly, a fidget, a delinquent. She had never been able to concentrate on school work but had stared out of the window towards the sea, dreaming of adventure.

She had volunteered for the Parents' Association with a rush of enthusiasm when her second child had joined the school, and was already regretting it. The meetings were formal and boring and the Association had none of the power she had imagined. It had been a rush to make a meal for Jim and the children and get to the school in time. Six o'clock was a most inconvenient time for a committee meeting, but Mr Medburn had insisted that it was the only time when he and his staff could attend. The committee knew that his object was to be as inconvenient as possible and had suggested that Mr Medburn's presence was hardly necessary. He, after all, had shown no enthusiasm for the formation of the Association. But he had stated that it would be impossible for them to use school premises without him, and the time had been agreed. As Patty entered the hall her depression deepened and she prepared to be bored.

Paul Wilcox was washing up and listening at the same time for the sound of his wife's car. From the living room came the voice of the television and occasionally the children's voices raised in argument. He supposed he should go into them and put an end to the quarrel. He should switch off the television and persuade them to play something constructive, but he was grateful to be on his own for a while.

They lived in a big house, converted from an old water mill, with a garden and a paddock by the stream. He had never expected to live in a house like that and it would have been impossible if he and not Hannah had been working. He loved the house, but it shamed him. It was a reflection of his incompetence. The kitchen, where he was hiding from the children, had a gloomy unfinished quality. It had a red quarry tile floor and a large dresser they had bought at an auction before the children were born, but some of the units were still without doors and it needed more light. Hannah thought that as he was home all day he should be able to turn the house into the dream property they had imagined it could be, but it was not that easy. He had worked as a nurse. He had never been a practical man. Besides he did not have Hannah's energy, her vitality, her ability to do three things at once and still do them all well.

He scraped remnants from Elizabeth's plastic plate into an already overflowing wastebin and wondered when he would have the courage to admit to Hannah that the experiment of role reversal had been a mistake. It had been his idea.

'You have a far greater earning potential than me,' he had said. She was a graduate, a mathematician. 'I'll enjoy being home with the children. It'll be exciting.'

Hannah had been unsure. She took motherhood seriously. She read books about it. Then an old colleague from the computer firm where she worked came to see her. He was considering setting up on his own, he said. A computer consultancy. There was a gap in the market in the north-east. Was she interested in joining him? For the first six months Paul worked nights while she struggled to make a go of it. She worked from home in the small terraced house where they lived. Elizabeth was a tiny baby and Joe a serious three-year-old. Then she started making money and to celebrate they moved to the old mill in Heppleburn and there was no longer any need for him to continue working.

At first it had been fine. It had been a joy to escape the routine of work. Joe was at nursery school and Elizabeth slept a lot. He planned the things he would do with his new free time. He would read, perhaps join a band again, decorate the mill, plant the garden. Then Elizabeth changed, almost overnight, into a kicking, screaming, demanding monster who drew in wax crayon on his books, broke the strings of his guitar and washed her hair in wallpaper paste. Their friends, said she was a normal toddler. Joe, they said, had been exceptionally good. They couldn't expect to have the same luck twice. For Paul the shock was enormous.

It would have been easier perhaps if they had family who lived locally, but they were both southerners and had no one to support them. Paul loved Heppleburn. It fitted in with all his romantic notions of the north. He liked the seamen's mission on the coast, the miners' welfare hall, the leek shows and the racing pigeons. He liked to talk to shop assistants and to old ladies in bus queues to show that he was friendly too. He and Hannah often told their friends from Kent about the day Hannah took Joe out in his pram as a new baby and the pram came back jingling with coins – the lucky money given by people in the street to celebrate his birth. But despite all that they had no real friends in the area. There was no one he could talk to.

As Hannah's business succeeded she came home later and stayed away more often. She was running courses, attending conferences, selling her skills. Some weeks Paul hardly saw her and at the weekends she was exhausted, kept awake only by nervous energy and her desire to have time with the children.

He joined the Parents' Association because it seemed the right thing to do. Some of his ideals about being the perfect parent still remained. He wanted to prove his commitment to Hannah but thought that she hardly noticed. He seemed to be losing her. She was slipping away from the family and he felt inadequate to take her place. Thousands of wives must feel like this, he thought as he looked at his watch again. He was so tight, so full of resentment, that he felt he should cry out to relieve the pressure. Perhaps then, magically, the self-pity would leave him like air from a balloon. It's my only night out this week and she's late.

Then he heard her car on the drive and the clang of the garage door and she was in the kitchen, her hands full of papers and files and a bulging briefcase. She was wearing a long, gaberdine mac which was crumpled because she had been sitting too long in the car. Her face was drawn and her eyes were grey and tired.

'I'm sorry I'm late,' she said, dropping everything in a heap on the kitchen table. 'It's those bloody road works on the A1. I'm so glad to be home.'

'Sit down,' he said, because it was impossible to be angry with her when she looked so small and ill. 'I'll make some tea.'

But as he filled the kettle he still wanted to cry or to scream as she started telling him about an awkward customer who had purposely misread the contract. He wanted to say that he had had a bad day too. He wanted to tell her about Lizzie wetting herself in the supermarket trolley and pulling the washing from the line into the mud, but he said nothing and pretended to be listening. Thousands of wives must feel like this, he thought again, but it was no real comfort.

'I'll have to go out now,' he said at last. She turned to him with a hurt bruised expression, so he realized he must have interrupted her.

'It's the Parents' Association,' he said defensively. 'I'm chairman. I'll have to go.' He would have liked to say something more to her, something intimate, fun even, telling her to be ready for him when he came home, but he knew she would not want to make love to him. She was too tired and would fall asleep as soon as they were in bed.

Outside the house he composed himself. He was determined to maintain the illusion that their life together was a success, that he enjoyed his role as a parent. Harold Medburn's remarks about his inability to support his family would not be allowed to hurt him this evening. He hurried up the lane towards the school and was the first one to arrive. When the others came into the hall he was already sitting in his place at the head of the table, studious, bespectacled and calm.

Irene Hunt unpinned the frieze of vegetables, flowers and fruit which the children had prepared for the Harvest Festival and threw it into the bin. It seemed ridiculous now that she had once had the ambition to be a student at the Royal School of Art. There was little sense of creativity in the visual arts form. After half term the bare space on the wall would be filled with the silhouettes of witches, cats and pumpkin lanterns. She did not entirely approve of Hallowe'en. It was, she thought, an American invention, but the children liked painting witches and it provided a focus for the craft work between Harvest and Bonfire Night. For forty years her life had been ruled by this calendar of childhood excitements and soon it would be over. At Christmas she would retire. For the last time she would teach her reception class to sing 'Away in a Manger', to perform the nativity play, to stick cotton wool onto black card in the shape of a snowman. It would be a relief to go. She had been forced into teaching by circumstance and though her disappointment had burned out long ago, she had never been fulfilled by it. It seemed to her that for the first time in her life she would have the opportunity to grow up, to become truly adult. She stood in front of the blackboard, a tall gaunt woman, and thought with pleasure that this would be the last parents' meeting she would have to attend.

The classroom door opened and Matthew Carpenter stood uncertainly on the threshold. When he had arrived as a new teacher at the school he had been full of enthusiasm and fun. There was little indication of that now.

'Come in,' she said. She was sorry for him and angry because of what Harold Medburn had done to him, but she was irritated too by his lack of fight and confidence in himself. Perhaps it was because she recognized something of herself in Matthew. She felt responsible for him. She should have had the confidence to stand up to Medburn years before. Well, she thought, soon she would be retired and there would be no need then for secrecy.

The arrival of Matthew Carpenter had marked the one major defeat Harold Medburn had suffered in his relations with the school governors. When a vacancy arose in the school he had wanted to appoint a middle-aged women, one of the congregation of St Cuthbert's Church where he was church warden. The governors decided that Mr Medburn's influence on the school was already too strong. It needed someone younger, with fresh ideas, someone more cooperative, more willing to involve the parents. Matthew Carpenter had been appointed straight from college knowing nothing of the problems he would face. From the moment of his arrival Harold Medburn set out to make his position there untenable. He criticized and contradicted the young teacher, so Matthew became confused and unhappy. His class recognized his increasing nervousness and grew unruly and noisy. Mr Medburn was exultant and some of the parents who had expected most from Matthew were beginning to complain about the lack of discipline.

'I don't want to disturb you,' Matthew said, but he went in and sat on one of the desks while she finished putting library books into piles for the next day. 'I don't know what I'll do when you leave.'

She looked at him. He seemed hardly more than a boy to her. He was long and thin with limbs that seemed to be jointed like a puppet's, a thin face and long bony fingers. His hair was curly and impossible to tidy, but he tried his best to please Medburn by being respectably, even soberly dressed.

I don't know what you'll do either, she thought. Some days she wondered if he would have some sort of breakdown. On those days Medburn would never leave him alone. The headmaster would pick at him like a bully with a weak and miserable child, using calculated jibes and warped sarcasm. At other times she thought Matthew would simply resign.

'You'll be all right,' she said. 'Just see out your probationary year. Then you can apply for something else. Besides, Mr Medburn won't be here for ever.'

'I'd leave,' he said suddenly, 'but my mother was proud when I became a teacher. It would upset her.'

It would upset me too, Irene Hunt thought. It would be a wicked, wicked waste.

Angela Brayshaw had the house to herself. She had taken her daughter to the home for elderly residents where her mother was proprietor and matron. She had not waited to speak to her mother – the place depressed her and she was feeling low enough already. Angela's house was tiny, one of the new terraces on the estate where Patty Atkins lived. She stood in the middle of the living room and felt trapped. Like a bird, she thought with an uncharacteristic flash of imagination, in a brick cage.

'I hate this place,' she said aloud. It was spotless, gleaming, but so poky, so unimpressive, so ordinary. She too was spotless and gleaming. Her blond hair shone silver. It was straight and beautifully cut. Her make-up was immaculate. She was small, wrapped in a big, black coat.

'I want more than this,' she cried to herself. 'I'd do anything to get away from here.'

Her husband had got away from it. Exhausted in the end by her ambition, her desire for the most expensive furniture, the newest car, the smartest clothes, he had left her. To Angela's incomprehension he had moved in with a plain, dowdy woman older than herself, who had two children and lived in a rundown cottage miles from anywhere. The role of deserted, injured wife had pleased Angela for a couple of months. The men in the neighbourhood helped do her garden and mended her car. Then she realized how poor she would be with only the maintenance and the supplementary benefit to live on, and she was angry and bitter. Before she had always had dreams to sustain her. David, her husband, would be promoted, he would earn more money, then they could move and she would have the sort of house she saw in soap powder advertisements on the television. There would be a kitchen big enough to dance in and a bathroom so grand that she would long for all her visitors to ask to use the lavatory. Now even Angela realized that in her present circumstances her dreams were unrealistic.

Well, she thought, and her face became stubborn and hard. Well, we'll just have to change the circumstances. She pulled her coat around her, shut the door and set out towards the school.

In the dining room in the school house Harold and Kitty Medburn had tea together. Kitty noticed how pleased he seemed with himself.

'I don't think young Carpenter will last much longer,' he said. 'He'll leave before Christmas. I knew he would never make a teacher. Perhaps now the governors will trust my judgement.'

'He'd probably do well enough,' she said, 'if you'd leave him alone.'

They seemed to argue all the time. In the beginning it had been a marriage of convenience. No one understood why she had married him. He had never been popular in the village, but he had suited her. She had fancied being a teacher's wife and knew he would never ask too much of her – to be available in bed of course, she had expected that – but not the closeness, the pretence of love, the cloying intimacy she saw in other couples and which would have been impossible for her. She wondered sometimes if there was something wrong with her. Perhaps it was unnatural to be so detached. If there had been children it might have been different, she would surely have felt something for her own offspring. But children had never come and she and Harold would live in the school house, having contact only when they argued and ate together, until he retired. It was the life she had chosen and she did not regret it.

'Are you working tonight?' he asked.

'Not till later,' she said. She was a district nurse and there were some old ladies to visit and settle for the night.

'I'll take a key then,' he said. 'I don't know when I'll be back. You know how these meetings go on.'

When Patty Atkins got into the hall the meeting had already started. The members sat with blank unlistening faces as the secretary read the minutes of the last meeting. There was the smell of school dinners and floor polish. Patty was suddenly determined that her idea for the Hallowe'en party would be discussed. Even if nothing came of it at least the monotony of the gathering would be broken. The meetings were usually entirely predictable. There would be a discussion about the distribution of produce from the Harvest Festival and the desirability of school uniform. Then there would be the ritual, unspoken, heartfelt prayer for the early retirement or sudden death of Harold Medburn.

Patty took her seat, stumbling as she did so over Angela Brayshaw's handbag, causing the secretary at the other end of the table to falter.

'Sorry,' Patty said, looking around at them all, grinning. It was impossible for her to be unobtrusive. She was too big, too clumsy, too interested in everyone. She had recently been for an unsatisfactory perm and her blonde hair was shaggy and difficult to manage. She was like a large and friendly dog.

The secretary glanced at Mr Medburn and continued reading nervously. The headmaster was a small, slight man with a head which seemed too big for his body, like a child's glove puppet. He had a bald head surrounded by a semicircle of grey tufts. His cheeks were round and red and he seemed at first to have an almost Dickensian good humour. His appearance was deceptive and everyone in the room was frightened of him.

Paul Wilcox called for the treasurer's report. Patty considered Paul with fascination and friendly amusement. He was so earnest and intense and his soft, southern voice always surprised her. He made her want to laugh. Yet the Wilcoxes represented a sophistication which she envied. They went to the theatre and their son had piano lessons. They lived in a big house and had a cleaning lady. She would like to know them better.

The treasurer began to read the accounts. Patty yawned and queried the expenditure of £10.14 for tea and coffee to relieve her boredom. The treasurer blushed indignantly and produced the receipts. The meeting droned on. The Harvest Festival was discussed. Parents congratulated the school on the quality of produce collected and asked if they might attend the celebration on the following year. The headmaster regretted that it was impossible but gave no excuse for his refusal. The other teachers were given no opportunity to comment.

Paul Wilcox stared unhappily at his agenda and asked if anyone had any other business for discussion. Patty looked up brightly from the scrap of paper where she was drawing a caricature of the headmaster.

'Yes,' she said. 'Why don't we have a social evening for the parents? Lots of other schools do it. Let's have a Hallowe'en party.'

The others looked at her with pity and admiration. They knew she only made these wild suggestions to shock. It had taken a special governors' meeting to persuade the headmaster to let the children have a Christmas party. He would never agree to parents enjoying themselves on school premises. There was a silence in which everyone expected Mr Medburn to invent a reason why such an occasion was impossible, but he did not speak. The chairman rubbed his beard uncertainly, cleared his throat and blinked.

'Well,' he said bravely. 'I must say that I'd be in favour of a social event. Anything that encourages parents to come into the school must be a good thing. What does anyone else think?'

The parents around the table avoided his eye. Was Mr Medburn's silence some sort of trap? If they backed Patty's proposal would he stare at them with his pebbly blue eyes and make them the object of his wrath and sarcasm?

'I think it's an excellent idea,' said Miss Peters. She was a temporary supply teacher, filling in during illness. She had nothing to lose.

'It does sound rather fun,' said the treasurer anxiously and there were muttered noises of agreement. Only Angela Brayshaw was silent. She never contributed to the meetings and Patty wondered why she had volunteered for the Association at all.

Paul Wilcox blinked and took a deep breath.

'What's your opinion, Mr Medburn?'

The headmaster shrugged as if he were above such triviality.

'Why not?' he said, then paused and stared unkindly at Patty before continuing, 'But I could only agree of course if Mrs Atkins is prepared to take responsibility for the organization. I couldn't expect my staff to give up their time.'

Patty was notorious for her lack of organization, but could sense the committee members willing her to reply positively.

'Of course,' she said, her imagination suddenly fired by the plan. It would be a magnificent party, she thought. The night would go down for ever in Heppleburn history. 'We'll ask everyone to come in fancy dress. We'll decorate the hall . . .'

'I'd like to volunteer to help with that,' Irene Hunt interrupted. 'Despite what Mr Medburn said, I'm quite prepared to give up my time.'

The chairman sensed the possibility of argument between the teachers. He was worried that they might lose the headmaster's limited approval.

'So you agree in principle, Mr Medburn,' he said quickly. 'As

Mrs Atkins has said she'll organize the event? And you will come yourself?'

'Oh yes,' the headmaster said unpleasantly. 'As it's to be arranged by these two admirable and competent women, I wouldn't miss it for the world.'

They ignored his sarcasm and discussed catering, hiring a bar and printing tickets until it was dark.

Jack Robson had come back to the school to lock up, and Patty waited for a quarter of an hour with him while he stacked the chairs ready for assembly the following day. Then they walked together down the hill towards the village.

It was a clear evening and they could see the lights of the ships at the mouth of the Tyne and the strings of neon on the front at Whitley Bay. At the end of the lane, hidden from the main road and the cars that passed by the hawthorn hedge, a man and a woman were locked in embrace. Even from a distance and in the distorting light from the street it was clear that these were not teenagers. They were obviously shocked by the sound of footsteps as Patty and Jack approached, and they separated, ran into the road and disappeared in opposite directions. Patty looked at her father.

'Wasn't that Angela Brayshaw and Harold Medburn?' she said.

'It could have been,' he said noncommittally.

'But he's married,' she blurted out. 'He's been married for years.'

'Don't you go gossiping,' Jack said. 'You don't know for certain it was Medburn.'

I know, she thought, remembering other meetings, the hand too long on her shoulder even when his words were most sarcastic, the way he looked at all the women there.

'I was at school with him, you know,' Jack said before he turned into his gate. 'There's more to that man then meets the eye.'

Chapter Two

They strung fairy lights along the outside of the school, so it looked from the village like a ship, stranded in a sea of brown fields. There was a full moon which rose behind the square tower of the church and made the playground as light almost as day, so they could see the printed squares for hopscotch on the concrete and the football posts in the field beyond. The yard was full of cars. The committee had sold more tickets than they ever expected. The village saw the party as a victory of the parents over Harold Medburn, and the women especially wanted to see him in defeat. They came dressed as witches with crepe-paper shirts and gaudy hats bought at the co-op in the village, harridans set to gloat over him. The men were embarrassed and soberly dressed and headed straight for the bar. They would rather have been in the club.

A small, unofficial sub-committee had been at the school for most of the day. It was a Saturday. There was Paul Wilcox, impractical and rather in the way, Angela Brayshaw who had surprised the committee by volunteering to supervise the catering for the event, and Jim and Patty Atkins. Patty had persuaded Jim to run the bar, but he was grumbling and ungracious because Newcastle United were playing at home. Patty was annoying the others with her arrogant assumption that she was in charge and the morning was chaotic and bad-tempered. When Miss Hunt arrived the mood changed.

Patty was prepared to relinquish control to her. They had been surprised when the teacher had volunteered to help decorate the hall – she was so dignified and stately, and Patty was unsure whether she would approve of the occasion. Yet she walked in at lunch-time, strange and unfamiliar in casual clothes, so they hardly recognized her, and she worked with them all afternoon.

They were amazed by her skill. She transformed the hall, not into a witch's cavern but a haunted house. In a rare moment of communication about her past she said that she had once had ambitions to be a theatre designer. She stuck ghosts and skeletons and a frieze of ravens on the walls and hung strings of paper bats from the ceiling. Most of the work was the children's, she said when they congratulated her on the effect. Witches had become rather clichéd and turnip lanterns would be impossible. Think of the fire risk, she said, and the smell of burning turnip always reminded her, for some reason, of scorching flesh.

In the afternoon Matthew Carpenter wandered in quite unexpectedly. He had taken no part until then in the arrangements. He seemed in desperate, almost hysterical good spirits and Patty suspected that he had been drinking. By then most of the work had been completed and there was little for him to do. The parents did not know how to talk to him. He was too young to receive the respect with which they approached the other teachers and yet they could hardly use the amused bantering tone in which they spoke to their older sons or nephews.

During the course of the afternoon he changed and became subdued and so preoccupied that he hardly seemed to notice them. He sat on the edge of a trestle table set up to form the bar and swung his legs like a moody teenager.

Harold Medburn's arrival late that afternoon was an anticlimax. They had been prepared for it, frightened that he would demolish their efforts with his words, but there was nothing, after all, to be worried about. He arrived, like visiting royalty, with smiles and congratulations. It was true that he seemed a little disappointed to learn that Angela Brayshaw had already gone home and when Paul Wilcox asked nervously if he might have a word in private, the headmaster said imperiously that he was far too busy, but that was only in character. When Medburn made his tour of inspection, Matthew Carpenter left the school with an abruptness that was obvious and rude. But the remaining committee members felt that the headmaster seemed pleased to have provoked such a reaction. He left after half an hour, jovial and beaming, promising to see them all later. They all went then to eat and change and prepare for the evening.

Jack Robson spent the evening in the small room which was hardly more than a cupboard where the cleaner kept her mops and buckets. It was his retreat. He had a kettle in there and a spare packet of Number Six in case he ran out, and a book. Although he had come to books late in life he needed them now as much as he needed cigarettes. He hoped the party would be a success for Patty's sake. She hadn't seemed settled since the bairns had started at school, and he found it hard to understand her recent aimlessness. He wished she were happier. When she was younger they had had their differences. She had been wilful and opinionated, and he had expected the same unquestioning respect which he had given his own father. Since his wife's death he and Patty had become very close. His friends had pitied his lack of sons, but he was pleased with his two daughters. He would have found it hard to express his love to boys. Susan, his eldest daughter, was clever and rarely came home. She worked as a secretary for an international company in Geneva. He admired her independence and was proud of her, but Patty was different. He was close to Patty. She was very like her mother.

Patty brought him a can of beer early in the evening. She wanted to thank him for his help and show off her costume. She saw him through cigarette smoke, a small grey man with big boots, squatting on a kitchen stool, buried in a biography of a First World War general. He wore baggy trousers which were too long for him and a hand-knitted jersey – the same sort of clothes his father had worn in the thirties. She bought him other clothes as presents but even when he put them on he always looked the same.

'It's a canny outfit,' he said, as if he had noticed her costume for himself and had not needed her to swing around to show him the long skirt and cloak. 'Is it a good evening?'

'It seems to be,' she said. She looked straight at her father. 'Medburn's not here yet. He promised he'd come.'

'He'll come if he said he would,' Jack said. 'He'll be late. He'll keep you all guessing.'

'It'll be a disaster if he doesn't come,' she said. 'Everyone's expecting him.'

'Away!' he said. 'By now everyone's enjoying themselves so much that they'll not notice.'

'I want him there,' she cried. She had been drinking wine and was excitable, showing off for him. 'I want him to see how well it's going. Otherwise he'll never admit I made it a success.'

'He'll be there,' Jack promised. He winked at her. 'I'll make sure he's there.'

Medburn owes me that much, Jack thought. He owes me enough to put in an appearance tonight to make my daughter happy. Jack was a year older than Medburn, but they had been to school together, to the school where Medburn was now headmaster. They had sat in different rows of the same classroom. Harry had been a fat, stodgy child, son of a clerk in the shipping office in Blyth, better off than most of them. He had been easily bullied but vicious when provoked to retaliation. No one had particularly liked him even then. And Jack had been at school with Kitty, Medburn's wife. He had loved Kitty Richardson with a passion which had astounded him as a young man and continued to catch him unawares. She had been a slight, small girl with the colouring of a red tabby cat and narrow green eyes. Perhaps Kitty had been a nickname, suggested by her appearance, though he could never remember her called anything else. He had a sudden picture of her in the school playground, ginger plaits dancing as she skipped with concentrated intensity, small red tongue gripped between her teeth. Jack was not sure how Harold Medburn had persuaded Kitty to marry him. He had been away on National Service; Harry for some forgotten reason had been exempted. But Jack was sure it was a kind of theft.

As soon as he opened the door to go into the corridor he could tell that the party was going well. Patty had hired a group of local musicians and he could hear the thumping rhythm of the music and laughter and talking. He was angered by the injustice of Medburn's absence. If none of the parents had turned up, if Patty had forgotten something important, the headmaster would have been there to gloat. Now he would stay away and pretend that it was beneath his dignity to join in.

In the hall Hannah and Paul Wilcox told each other that it was the best evening they had enjoyed for years. This was one of the reasons why it was so good to live in the north-east, they said self-consciously, drinking Newcastle Brown Ale from plastic mugs. There was a sense of community to be found nowhere else. How they pitied their friends who still lived in the Home Counties! The conversation made Paul uneasy. It was a complacent charade. When they first met they would have been more honest. It would have been easier then to tell Hannah about Angela Brayshaw. Hannah's fierce directness had once taken his breath away; she had been tactlessly truthful. Now they were like the middle-aged couples they had despised.

'I need to have you around more,' he said suddenly, staring into the thick brown beer. 'I can't manage on my own.'

'Nonsense,' Hannah said. She sounded amused. She was trying to ignore the desperation in his voice. He wanted to make some grand outrageous gesture to show her how depressed he felt. 'Nonsense. You've managed fine. Lizzie will be at playgroup soon. Then you'll have more time to yourself.'

'I don't want more time to myself,' he cried. 'I need company. I need your company.'

'How sweet you are!' she said. She bent over the table to kiss his forehead. He could tell that she was still tired and did not have the energy to take him seriously. It was no time for revelation.

'Come and dance,' he said. He took her hand and they joined the crowd under the flashing lights at the centre of the hall. The crowd parted to let them through, then gave them room to move because they danced so well. Everything we do is a sort of performance, Paul thought. We pretend to be a perfect couple. Why can't we be natural with each other any more? Why can't we say what we think? At one time he had always known what she was thinking. Now, even when they were making love he could tell that her mind was elsewhere, perhaps with her accountant or at the next sales conference or with her smart, grey-suited partner. If only he were brave enough to talk to her, he thought. That might bring them closer together again. But Medburn was right. He was too scared to take the risk.

Jack looked through the glass door into the hall. He was reminded of the old days when Susan and Patty had been allowed to youth club dances and he had been sent by Joan to walk them home safely. There was the same feeling of being excluded from their pleasure. 'I can't get no satisfaction,' the group sang and he supposed that this noise held the same sentimental associations for Patty and her contemporaries as big bands did for him. He saw Angela Brayshaw sitting at a small table by the bar drinking a glass of wine. She was alone and seemed quite detached from the general good humour.

She held the glass daintily to her mouth like some amateur actress portraying a duchess drinking tea. She saw him looking at her and smiled, flattered as she was by any male attention – even that of someone as unlovely as Jack Robson. He turned away, reminded suddenly and unreasonably of Kitty Medburn.

Jack pushed open the heavy arched door into the playground. Outside it was very cold. Through the uncurtained window he could see the shapes of dancing witches and ghosts, their costumes becoming more bedraggled as the evening went on. Suddenly the new, young teacher stumbled out of the door behind him. He stood still, bent double, his hands on his knees as if he might be sick.

'Are you all right, lad?' Jack said. Matthew straightened up, pulled himself together.

'Yes thank you,' he said, forming the words with unnatural and forced precision. 'It was just a bit hot in there.'

And he fled back to the hall and the bar. He'll have to be careful, Jack thought. Medburn's only looking for an excuse to sack him. If he shows himself up tonight he'll be in real trouble. He hesitated, wondering if he should follow Matthew and offer to take him home, but he continued over the playground to the school house where the Medburns lived, his boots ringing on the tarmac in the clear air.

He could still hear the music and it annoyed him to think that Medburn, in his living room, must be able to hear it too. He had never been in the Medburns' house. He had lived in the same village as Kitty for sixty years, yet since her marriage he had scarcely spoken to her. She had come occasionally to nurse his wife. Even in her anonymous uniform and despite his anxiety and guilt, he had been intensely aware of her, but she had seemed not to recognize him. After her marriage to Medburn they had moved in different circles and he had given all his loyalty and affection to his wife.

He knocked at the door of the school house. There was no light in the living room and the curtains were still undrawn. Standing there, as he had stood many times, waiting for instructions about light bulbs to be replaced or lavatory paper to be ordered, he tried desperately to maintain his anger. He knocked again, more loudly and impatiently, and stamped his boots on the step. A light went on in the passage and a door was opened. Kitty was standing there and he could tell at once that something was wrong. She was still wearing her district nurse's uniform and she was expecting someone else.

'Jack?' she said. 'Jack Robson. Is it you?' She peered at him, though she must have been able to see with the light from the corridor thrown out onto the yard.

'Aye,' he said. 'I've come to see why you and Harold aren't at the Parents' Association Hallowe'en party. I thought something might be wrong.'

'Of course,' she said. 'The party. I wondered what that music was. I'd forgotten all about it.'

'Can I come in?' Jack said. She seemed so vague and so different that he thought she must be ill.

She stood aside and let him walk past. She must have come in from work hours before but the house was cold. He walked into a small back room where a fire was laid in a grey tile grate. It was a shabby, miserable room, he thought. There was a dark wallpaper and heavy furniture.

'Where's Harold?' he asked. She had followed him into the room without a word. Her hair was shorter and curled softly about her face and it still had traces of copper in the grey. Her face was blank, but there were tears on her cheeks. He had never known her cry, even as a girl.

'I don't know,' she said. 'He went out earlier. I don't know if he'll be coming back.'

He went up to her and put his arm around her. It was a friendly gesture of comfort but as he touched her he knew he would never be satisfied with friendship.

'What do you mean,' he said gently, 'that Harold won't be coming back?'

'We had a row,' she said. He could imagine her in bitter arguments. She would be a fighter. In the playground she had kicked and punched as hard as the boys. 'We have a lot of arguments.'

'He'll be back,' Jack said, easy, reassuring. 'He would never leave you.'

'He's got another woman,' she said. 'He told me when he was angry. He said he wanted to live with her, not with me. Then he had a phone call and he went away.'

She spoke simply. He could not tell if she were angry or unhappy.

'But what about the party?' Jack cried. 'What about Patty's Hallowe'en party?'

'Perhaps he's forgotten about it too,' she said.

She released herself from his arm and sat on an overstuffed settee.

'I was jealous,' she said. 'We've had our rows, but I didn't want anyone else to have him. Especially someone younger. I'm used to him. I'm too old for change.' She hesitated and he thought she was going to say something more.

'No,' he said. 'We're not too old at all.'

She stood up.

'You'd better go,' she said. 'You'll miss your party.'

He had been surprised that she had confided in him. He realized now that she was already regretting it. More than anything he wanted her to trust him.

'You've no idea,' Jack said, 'where he is?'

She shook her head. 'I thought it must be his woman friend on the telephone', she said quietly. 'I presume he's gone to her.'

No, Jack thought, remembering Angela Brayshaw's smile. That's impossible. She's in the school.

Kitty opened the front door to let him out. He could hear the music again and saw dark silhouettes of people swirling against the spotlights inside. He was reminded of the *Titanic*, of the passengers who laughed and danced and drank champagne, unaware of imminent tragedy. He turned to say something else to Kitty, but she was gone and the door was firmly closed. He was disappointed – he'd thought he might take her hand before he went, to remind her of his support – but he could understand that she was too proud to share her unhappiness with him.

On the way back to the school across the short space of the playground he was as confused and excited as a boy. There had been, between him and Kitty, an intimacy which he would never have thought possible. He was thrilled because she had not treated him as a stranger – she had chosen to tell him about Harold Medburn's affair when there had been no need to. At the same time he felt guilty, as if this excitement were a betrayal of his affection for Joan, his wife, a rejection of the calm support she had given him throughout their marriage.

At the door into the school he paused. He wanted more time to savour the memory of the conversation with Kitty, to assess for himself if the significance he had given to it was real. He needed to be alone, away from the noise of the party. There was a small walled playground at the side of the school, used exclusively by the younger children, so they would not be frightened by the rowdiness of the older boys. It was as bleak and sunless, he always thought, as the exercise yard of a prison, a depressing place for the infants to play, but he knew he would be private there. The wooden door set in the wall opened by a latch. He was surprised by how silently and smoothly it opened, and walked through.

Set in the wall at one end of the yard was a rusting netball hoop. It had been there as long as he could remember, and when the school had taken pupils until the age of fourteen it had been used by the older girls. It was too high for the younger children. As he walked into the yard, trying again to conjure Kitty's face, her voice, her presence, the moon was directly above him and filled the walls with its white light. It left little shadow. The only shadow was on the concrete under the netball hoop and it moved as the figure above it, which hung from the loop and threw the shadow, swung very gently.

At first Jack thought it was some tattered remnant of the party, a giant bat with folded wings, discarded as being too grotesque even for Hallowe'en. Then, as the figure turned on its axis, he saw it was Harold Medburn, wrapped in his academic gown, hanging from a noose made of white pieces of cloth. The contrast of black and white and the gloss of the moonlight turned the picture into a strip of negative film, just pulled from the photographer's fluid. He shut the door on it and stood for a moment in the playground.

The party was over. There were loud shouts of farewell and the noise of banging car doors and engines.

At least Medburn didn't spoil Patty's evening, he thought, before he even wondered why the headmaster had hanged himself or realized that now Kitty would be free.

It was only much later, when the police came with their questions and cars and spotlights, that he was told that Medburn had been murdered.

Chapter Three

Saturday night was a bad time for murder, especially in Northumberland, where serious crime was rare. The divisional commander was at a dinner dance but was so shocked by the news of the murder that he sobered immediately. Ramsay was the only detective inspector the Otterbridge Communications Centre could contact, and he was in bed. No one knew where to find the portable generators to power the spotlights and when they were tracked down it took some time to find the keys to the storeroom. Detective Sergeant Hunter, who was supposed to be on duty, was not answering the radio. As the unfamiliar first steps of a murder inquiry were taken, Medburn's body swung from the netball hoop, waiting for the photographer, and for the senior policemen to come to a decision about how the investigation should progress.

The commander, the superintendent from Otter-bridge and Ramsay stood in the moonlight on the frosty playground, unwilling participants in the Hallowe'en drama. The commander had been moved from the city centre division to wind down before retirement. He had been a good policeman in his day, everyone admitted, but was more adept at public relations now than catching criminals. The superintendent was a fat and idle man whose limited energies were devoted to his hobby of amateur dramatics. In the end they left it all to Ramsay. He would carry out the investigation after all.

'Delegation,' the superintendent muttered to himself as he walked back to his car. 'That's the secret of good management.'

More importantly Ramsay was unpopular and if anyone was to make a mistake it would better be him.

The inspector watched them make their excuses and scurry away. He knew better than to expect their support. He had no illusions about his work.

The commander went home to bed, to sleep off the effect of too much food and whisky, and Ramsay was left alone with the uniformed policeman who was guarding the gate to the playground. Ramsay was a tall, angular figure in a long overcoat and he waited without moving.

Later the young constable told his friends that he was more spooked by the motionless, silent figure of the inspector than by the body still wrapped in the bat-like gown. It was dawn before the civilian scene-of-crime officer arrived and Ramsay finally allowed the the body to be removed. It was dawn before Gordon Hunter, cocksure and unrepentant, turned up in a taxi.

If Kitty Medburn had not been given sedation, Ramsay would have spoken to her first and the relationship with Patty Atkins might not have become so central to the case. In the event Patty was first alphabetically on the list of suspects, and Ramsay was aware, almost immediately, that she could be useful to him. She was bright, curious, involved in the community. She spoke without thinking and wanted to please them. At first he set Gordon Hunter to charm her. Hunter was young, attractive in a brash way, appealing, Ramsay thought, to women. But as they sat in her living room, with Hunter asking the questions, Ramsay came to realize that she was performing for *him*. Hunter was asking the questions but when she came to answer she faced the corner where Ramsay was sitting. This came as a shock to the inspector. Since his wife had left him some months before he had avoided the company of women. He had no intention of making a fool of himself again. Yet even on that first meeting there was an understanding between the bored, disorganized housewife and the aloof, rather arrogant policeman, which would dictate the course of the investigation. They liked each other from the beginning.

'Come on, love,' Hunter said, smiling, showing no indication that he had spent the night drinking. 'You knew Harold Medburn. Tell us about him. Anything would be useful.'

She had hesitated and glanced towards Ramsay who nodded in encouragement. Later her father was to ask her what she saw in Ramsay and she did not know what to say. He was middle-aged, dark, so tall he seemed to have an habitual stoop. Yet she felt from the beginning that his approval was worth having. He was a man of judgement. If he showed that he had confidence in her she would have confidence in herself. So, quite quietly, with none of her usual melodrama, she told the policemen about Medburn's affair with Angela Brayshaw. She was rewarded by Ramsay's smile.

She only learned later, from her father, that Kitty Medburn had been taken into custody.

Jack Robson was beside himself with fury.

In the afternoon he walked with Patty on the empty sandy beach at the end of the valley. Jim had taken the children to his mother's and Patty had insisted that she needed fresh air.

'I want to talk to you,' Jack said angrily. As soon as he heard of Kitty's arrest he had stormed to her house and banged on the door, ignoring the enjoyment of the neighbours.

'You can talk just as well outside.'

She had not slept and her eyes felt tight with tiredness. The sea was grey despite the sunshine, and a strong east wind blew sand around their ankles and flattened the marram grass against the dunes. They walked from the car park through the dunes to the flat hard shore.

'What did you do it for?' he demanded. 'Why did you have to tell the police?'

'Why not?' she said defensively. 'They would have found out anyway.'

'No,' he said. 'They needn't have done. Who was going to tell them? Not me. I'd not tell them anything. Not Angela Brayshaw. She's too sly to get herself involved with the police.'

'But if Kitty killed her husband,' Patty said, stung to anger, 'the police had to find out.'

28

They walked in silence. Patty had a hangover and the waves breaking on the beach echoed her thumping head. She pulled her thick padded jacket around her. She felt drained and ill.

'You never told me,' she said at last, sulky as a schoolgirl. 'You never told me to keep quiet about it.'

'You shouldn't need telling!' Jack said. His anger and unhappiness floated undirected over the sea. He could not really blame Patty.

He was wearing a long grey macintosh, exactly the same as the one he had bought after leaving the army, and his Sunday black shoes. He looked out of place: a Raymond Chandler detective on a Northumberland beach. All he needed was a hat. He had never enjoyed the beach. He had come there a lot with his dad when he was a boy, not playing like Patty's children in the summer with buckets and spades, but for the fishing and to see what they could find washed up on the tide line. The water was beginning to seep into his shoes and he felt cold, though he would never admit it to her.

'If Kitty Medburn had killed her husband,' he said more quietly, 'she would have told me so last night.'

'You went to see her last night?'

He nodded. 'I went to find out why they weren't at the party.'

'What did she say?' Patty was fascinated. She still thought Kitty Medburn was a murderess. There was a ghoulish curiosity about the meeting.

'She'd had a row with Harold. He said he was going to leave her for another woman. Then he had a phone call and he went out.'

'What time?'

'I don't know,' he said. 'Early in the evening. When she came in from work, I suppose.'

'So she could have killed him,' Patty said. 'The school was empty between five o'clock and seven. The noose was made from bandages. She was a district nurse, she would have had bandages at home. The police said that. They think it was a dreadful sick joke, a way of paying him back for his infidelity.'

'No,' he said. 'She might have killed him in a temper, but she would never have gone through all that charade. She would have told me when I went there that evening.'

'How do you know?' she demanded. 'Why are you such an expert on Kitty Medburn's state of mind?'

'I used to know her.' It was his turn to be defensive. 'She was a friend. Before I met your mother.'

She could tell that there was little point in asking more questions about this mysterious friendship. He turned to face the sea and they watched the white shape of the Norway Line's *Jupiter* move out of the mouth of the Tyne on its way to Scandinavia, the white gulls hovering over her.

'Did the police tell you how he died?' Jack asked. 'They would tell me nothing.'

'No,' she said. 'They say they're waiting for the results of the post mortem.'

'You seem to have got on very well with them,' he said.

'And why not? They're not some kind of enemy.' But as she spoke she thought she couldn't be sure about that. There was something dangerous about the policeman who sat in the corner. It was hard to forget him.

Jack turned again towards the sea.

'Medburn mightn't have been a big man,' he said. She knew he was trying to persuade himself, not her, of Kitty's innocence. 'But she would never have been able to carry him from the house to the playground.'

'She could have killed him in the school,' Patty said. She felt spiteful because of his hurtful comments. 'That's what the police said. Or they think she could have moved him in a wheelchair. She had one at home because of her work.'

'He *was* dead when he was strung up like that?' Jack asked sharply. 'Did your friends from the police tell you that?'

'I don't know,' she said. She began to sob quietly. 'I don't want to think about it any more. It's too horrible.'

He put his arm around her and pulled her head onto his shoulder. 'Now pet,' he said, as he had when she was a baby. 'Don't cry!' They walked back to the car. He bought coffee from a van parked by the side of the road and they sat in the car looking over the dunes down to the beach.

'I'm sorry,' he said. 'I shouldn't have shouted at you. I was worried about Kitty.' He hesitated. 'I was very fond of her.'

She had mopped up her tears and was looking with horror at her red, blotchy face in the car mirror. She was determined to be sensible. 'Well,' she said. 'There's nothing we can do to help her: We'll have to leave it to the police now.'

'But she's no friends!' he cried. 'No one to speak up for her.'

'The police will get her a solicitor.'

'It won't be the same,' he said. 'He won't know her. I feel responsible. I should have stayed with her last night.'

'What good would that have done?' Patty said. 'Medburn was already dead then.'

'I can help her now,' Jack said with an outrageous gallantry which left her breathless. 'I can find out who killed Medburn.'

'Don't be ridiculous, Dad!' she said. 'That's a job for the police. What could we do?'

He was encouraged by the 'we'. Joan had always supported him, even when she thought he was wrong. Independence had come hard to him and he needed Patty now.

'We could talk to people,' he said. 'We know them. Where do the police come from? Otterbridge? They know nothing about Heppleburn. We know what a bastard Harold Medburn was, and we know how many people hated him.' He looked at his daughter. 'You could talk to Angela Brayshaw,' he said. 'She's a neighbour of yours. That would be a start. Find out what she was getting from that relationship with Medburn. She wasn't doing it for love.'

'Oh Dad!' she said. 'I don't even like her. I wouldn't know what to say.'

'For Christ's sake!' He shouted so loud that a woman walking past the car turned and stared at them. 'You're always telling me there's no purpose to your life and you're sick with boredom. Well, I'm giving you a purpose. We're going to prove that Kitty Medburn was innocent.'

He knew that she would agree to do as he said. She would agree to anything that was different, a bit of excitement, an excuse to let the housework slide for a few days. She turned to him.

'Are you sure,' she said, 'that Kitty is innocent?'

'Of course,' he said uncomfortably, but they both knew that there was no certainty and that the thing would probably end in embarrassment and disaster.

As she stood on Angela Brayshaw's doorstep, dishevelled from the wind, with sand still on her boots, Patty realized that she should have gone home and changed first. Then perhaps she would not have felt at such a disadvantage. Angela was as calm and immaculate as ever. She opened the door only wide enough to see who was there.

'Yes?' she said distantly. 'What can I do for you?'

Patty might have been there to borrow sugar or sell insurance. There was no recognition in Angela's face, no indication that they had shared an experience of such horror as the discovery of Medburn's body.

'Can I come in?' Patty said, stamping her feet on the path in a vain attempt to shift the sand from her boots. 'I'd like to talk to you.'

It was already growing dark and lights were coming on in the other houses in the street. Angela could see the flickering images of colour television sets, the peering faces as neighbours, who had seen policemen call at the house earlier in the day, hoped for further excitement.

Reluctantly Angela moved aside to let Patty into the room. She was wearing a black skirt which reached to the middle of her calves and a black and white blouse. Her face was smooth, discreetly made up. She stood quite still and waited for Patty to speak.

'Where's Claire?' Patty asked. The children were something they had in common. Angela's daughter and Jennifer were friends.

'She's at my mother's,' Angela said. 'She stayed there last night so I could be at the school. She's better off there today. I don't want her troubled by this unpleasantness.'

She spoke as if murder were a trivial inconvenience. Patty stood awkwardly, unsure how to go on. The room was hot and she felt suddenly flushed. Perhaps she should make some excuse about having called to see how Angela was, then leave. But she thought of her father, waiting at her home, desperate for some information which would dramatically prove the innocence of the woman Patty realized, now, she knew little about. She sat resolutely on the small grey sofa.

'Have the police been to see you?' she asked.

Angela looked at her, unoffended but disapproving. She wished Patty would go away. She did not want to be reminded of the police or Harold Medburn. She wanted to forget about that now. And how big and clumsy Patty was, with that shapeless old coat and long scarf! She seemed to take up all the space in the room. Yet it was impossible for Angela to cause a scene, to tell Patty that it was none of her business. She sat, tense and upright, on a chair with her back to the window.

'Yes,' she said. 'They were here this morning.'

It had been a surprise when Ramsay and Hunter arrived and began, almost at once, to ask about her relationship with Harold Medburn. She had thought she had managed to keep the thing secret. The knowledge that the village was discussing her, grinning, as the young policeman had grinned at the thought of the two of them together, she young and beautiful, Medburn unpopular and unattractive, was worse almost than the indignity of having to answer the policeman's questions. She had got rid of them as quickly as she could and given away as little as possible.

'I saw you with Harold Medburn on the evening of the committee meeting,' Patty said. 'I told the police.'

Angela stared at Patty with expressionless blue eyes.

'I thought it might be you,' she said.

'I'm sorry,' Patty said. 'It seemed important. I didn't think until later how awkward it might be for you.'

'No,' Angela said bitterly, showing emotion for the first time. 'You never *do* think, do you? It's easy for you with your husband and your family and your friends in the village. That's all you want.

You've got everything you need. You never think of people like me. I hate it in Heppleburn.'

It's not all I want, Patty thought, but it was not the time to explain her problem. She had been shocked by Angela's outburst. She felt that the woman hated her and she wanted to make things better between them. She was accustomed to being liked.

'I'm sorry,' she said again. 'It must have been a dreadful shock when Harold Medburn died. Especially when you were so close to him.'

Angela did not reply immediately. She stared, and for a moment Patty wondered if she had said the wrong thing again. Angela thought at first that Patty might be sneering at her, laughing at her liaison with Medburn, but Patty seemed so earnest and confused that it was impossible after all to doubt her sincerity.

'Yes,' Angela said. 'It was a shock.'

There was another silence. The gas fire hissed and outside the street lamps came on with a sudden orange light. In a moment of weakness, caused by her tiredness and the other woman's sympathy, Angela felt she wanted to talk about Harold Medburn. She wanted Patty to understand about him, in a way that the police with their intimate, tasteless questions had been unable to. Since she had left school she had been without friends. Patty, with her intrusive good will, was the best she had.

'I thought Harold could give me something different,' she said. 'I want more than this.'

Patty followed her gaze around the square little room. The house was smaller than her own home, but Angela had made it stylish. It seemed more spacious than it was.

'It's fine,' she said encouragingly. 'It's big enough for the two of you.'

'No,' said Angela crossly, frustrated because she could not find the words to explain. 'I don't just mean the house . . .'

She wanted to tell Patty that she aspired to a certain dignity, to a lifestyle that did not involve struggling for every penny, making do with second best.

'I've not got any skills,' she said at last. 'I can't go out and earn a good living. All I've got is the way I look and the fact that men find me attractive.'

There was a pause.

'You mean you went with Harold Medburn for money?' Patty asked. She could think of no tactful way of putting it. She was shocked, not by Angela's confession, but because she had never guessed. Everyone on the estate thought that Angela led a life of great respectability.

'I don't usually take money,' Angela said.

'Oh,' said Patty, perhaps a little disappointed.

Angela looked at her again with clear blue eyes. 'I take other things,' she said. 'I take meals in good restaurants, trips to the theatre, clothes. From Harold Medburn I could have taken marriage.'

'You would never have married him!' Patty cried, shocked to indiscretion. 'What could you have seen in him?'

'Comfort,' Angela said. 'He had a lot of money, you know. More than you'd realize. He'd a lot saved and he'd not spend it on himself. He'd have bought me a nice house and furnished it as I wanted.' She hesitated. 'He loved me.'

She thought, with a vivid horror, of his leering face, his insistent pressing hands, his moist tongue, and was glad that he was dead.

'He loved me,' she repeated calmly. 'He said he would leave his wife for me.'

'Would you have married him?' Patty asked. The thing seemed to her inconceivable, grotesque, like the fable of Beauty and the Beast.

'I don't know,' Angela said. Then she seemed to reconsider. 'No,' she said. 'I don't think I could have married him.' But there are worse things, she thought, than marriage to Harold Medburn.

'Did you tell him that?'

Angela shook her head. 'I hoped when it came to it, he wouldn't be able to leave his wife.'

'Last night he'd made up his mind to leave her.'

They looked at each other. Both were amazed at the ease with which Angela had confided in Patty. They felt that they had known

35

each other for a long time and that each was being entirely honest. Yet they still disliked each other.

'Did you phone Mr Medburn yesterday evening?' Patty asked. 'After we had left the school at half past four?'

'No,' Angela said. 'The police asked me that. I never phoned him at home.'

'Were you expecting to see him at the party?'

'Yes,' Angela said. 'He'd told me that he wanted to dance with me.' She gave a slight shudder, as if she were cold. 'I was glad,' she said, 'when he didn't turn up.'

'Do you think his wife killed him because she was jealous?'

'I don't know,' Angela said. She seemed almost indifferent. 'Who else would have done it?'

'Nobody liked him,' Patty said. 'Everyone with kids at the school wanted rid of him.' She paused. 'Had there been any other women before you?'

'Probably,' Angela said. 'He was that sort of man.'

'Was there someone in Heppleburn?'

'He never talked about it,' Angela said. 'He wanted me to think I was special, the first apart from his wife. In a way it was true. He might have had other women but I *was* special. He wanted me. I was the only person he was willing to spend money on. You know how mean he was. He would have done anything for me.' She spoke in the same matter-of-fact voice but added bitterly, 'At least, nearly anything.'

'What do you mean?'

'Oh,' she said, 'A couple of weeks ago, the night you saw us after the meeting, I asked him for a favour. He wouldn't take me seriously.'

'What sort of favour?'

'Nothing important,' Angela said. 'It doesn't matter now. I would probably have got my way in the end.'

But Patty had the impression that it had mattered, very much, and there was an edge of triumph in Angela's voice which suggested that she had got the better of Harold Medburn, after all.

Outside it was beginning to get dark and the wind scattered the first brown leaves from the sycamore trees in the street. Angela stood up and pulled together the grey nylon velvet curtains. It was an indication that she wanted Patty to go, but Patty refused to take the hint.

'Do you know who might have killed him?' she asked.

'No,' Angela said. 'Of course not.' Then she added maliciously, 'You could ask Miss Hunt. She's a nosy old cow and she never liked him.'

'How do you know?'

Angela shrugged. 'Oh,' she said, 'from some of the things he said.' She went to a cupboard under the stairs and pulled out her coat. 'I'll have to go to my mother's. She'll be expecting me. She's busy at weekends. None of the staff want to work on Sundays.'

'I'd better go then,' Patty said, but still did not stand up. She wanted to be sure that she had asked all the important questions. She knew that the opportunity would not arise again. Already Angela was speaking in her polite, distant voice, as if there had never been any intimacy between them.

'There's nothing else you can tell me about Mr Medburn?' Patty said.

'No,' Angela said. 'He was very secretive about a lot of his life.'

Patty stood up, buttoned her coat, wound the scarf around her neck.

'I'll go now,' she said, 'and let you get off to your mam's.'

She waited for the other woman to open the door, but now it was Angela's turn to hesitate.

'Why are you asking all these questions?' she asked. 'What has it to do with you?'

Patty was going to say that she had no special interest, that she was only being friendly, but she thought that Angela deserved honesty too.

'Kitty Medburn is an old friend of my father's,' she said. 'He wants to prove that she's innocent.'

Angela nodded her understanding.

'I didn't kill Harold,' she said. 'You can tell your father that. I'm not sorry he's dead, but I didn't kill him.'

Then she opened the door and let Patty out into the dark street. Patty walked home the long way, along the footpath by the burn past the old mill. She wanted to be alone to savour the exhilaration of the successful interview with Angela Brayshaw. She had achieved more than she had expected. She had never thought that Angela would speak to her so freely. There was nothing definite of course, nothing which would lead directly to Medburn's murderer, but Patty thought that Jack would be pleased with her.

On the recreation field by the burn a huge bonfire had already been built in preparation for Firework Night. The bonfire was an annual event in Heppleburn. Patty supposed that they would bring the children to see the firework display, though now it seemed hard to imagine that life in the village would continue as normal. She certainly felt different. Her ability to persuade Angela to talk to her had given her a new confidence. She was determined, as she walked along the windy path, that she and her father would discover the identity of Harold Medburn's murderer. She needed to succeed at something.

As she walked past the old mill she looked in and even from the road, across the garden, she could see the whole family, like toys in a doll's house. None of the curtains were drawn. It was a sort of arrogance, Patty thought. It indicated that the family had nothing to hide, that they did not care whether or not the world knew their business. Upstairs Hannah Wilcox was working at a desk by the window. Her face was caught in the light of an anglepoise lamp, and Patty thought she had probably been working there all day. In a large room downstairs the children sat on the carpet in front of the television. The set was on, but they were not watching it. They were squabbling, fighting over a picture book. In the same room, but ignoring the quarrelling children, Paul Wilcox stood by the window and stared out into the dark garden. She hurried past and quickly turned her head away in case he should see her looking in and think she was prying.

In fact he saw nothing. The road was dark and he was deep in thought.

In the big house there seemed to be no contact between the

inhabitants. The children fought out of boredom and the adults were concerned with private problems. Patty wondered how she could ever have thought that the Wilcoxes were glamorous. That evening they seemed lonely and rather pathetic. The thought that her own family life was preferable to theirs made her feel stronger, more content. She hurried home quickly to see Jim and the children and to tell her father what had happened. In the village, walking briskly away from her, she saw Ramsay. She almost ran up to him and told him what she had discovered from Angela Brayshaw, but a sense of loyalty to her father, and the thought that the policeman would find her foolish, prevented her.

Angela Brayshaw drove her Mini through the stone gateway and parked in front of Burnside, the house which she had considered her own home since she was a child. When her parents had bought it the place had been a guest house, rundown and shabby, with very few residents. It had been bought cheap. Her father had done all the building, the repair and the plumbing to turn it into her mother's dream of a nursing home for the elderly. Uncharitable neighbours said that Mrs Mount had killed her husband with her nagging. He had worn himself out with all the work.

It was a square, angular house built of an unpleasant mustard-coloured brick. There were no trees or shrubs near the building. Mrs Mount was afraid of leaves in the drainpipes, roots in the foundations, dirt and expense.

As she locked her car Angela could hear the television. It was always turned up so loud that even the deafest of residents could hear it. She could picture the room, plain and antiseptic, the vinyl-covered chairs against each of the four walls, the silent staring faces.

Mrs Mount must have been listening for the car because as soon as Angela opened the door she was there, smooth and ageless, smelling of disinfectant and talcum powder.

'Well,' Mrs Mount said. 'What's been going on? I've been hearing nothing but rumours all day.'

'Oh Mam,' Angela said. 'Let me in. It's cold out here and I'm tired.'

Inside, two old people with walking frames were racing for the only vacant toilet. One was a man, tall and skeletal, with bony cheek and hands like claws. The other was a tiny woman. They jostled down the corridor, banging the paintwork with their frames. The race was in deadly earnest; neither spoke or smiled. When the woman reached the toilet first the man howled obscenities at her.

'Not now, Mr Wilson,' Mrs Mount said in her nanny's voice. 'There's no need for such a fuss. I'm sure Miss Watkins won't take long.'

In her triumph Miss Watkins had forgotten to close the lavatory door and they could see her sitting there, her skirt bunched around her thighs, frail legs dangling like a child's.

'I hear the police were at your house,' Mrs Mount said. 'It is true that Mr Medburn's dead?'

Angela nodded.

'Why did the police come to you?'

'Because I was at the school on the night he died.' She had been dreading these explanations.

'Of course,' Mrs Mount said. Her face was wrinkle-free, complacent. Inside the nursing home it was very hot and her skin glowed, as if she had completed some vigorous exercise. 'I've been hearing rumours,' she said, 'about you and Mr Medburn. They can't be true?'

'Oh Mam,' Angela said. 'Of course not.' She was twelve again, pretending to be good, pretending that it was the other girls who started nastiness, other girls who told lies.

'Of course not,' Mrs Mount repeated. 'I told them: "My Angela's no gold-digger," I said. "She might have had financial problems, but we've sorted them out now. I'm dealing with her debts and she's going to help me out in the nursing home in return.".' She turned to her daughter. 'It'll be like the old times,' she said. 'You and I working together again.'

'Perhaps,' Angela said evasively. 'I wish you wouldn't tell the whole of Heppleburn about my financial problems.'

Mrs Mount seemed not to have heard.

'Come into my room,' she said. 'I've been looking through those bills you gave me. I'm sure we can sort it all out. Claire's in with the residents watching the television. They do enjoy her company.'

Mrs Mount led her into the small flowered and scented room which was part office, part parlour, where she presided over her empire. Against one wall was a piano, whose lid had never been opened in Angela's lifetime. In a cage on a stand a budgerigar slept.

'Margaret!' Mrs Mount shouted and a young woman in a white overall appeared at the door. 'Bring us some tea dear, will you.'

The woman disappeared and Mrs Mount turned to her daughter.

'Now dear,' she said. 'When do you think you'll be able to start work here? It would be easier, don't you think, if you and Claire moved back to live.'

'No,' Angela said firmly. 'Whatever happens we'll keep our own home.'

'Only if the mortgage is paid, dear. You know what the building society said . . . I was happy to settle the arrears but that was a considerable sum even for me to find. I don't think I'd be able to do it again.' Mrs Mount smiled but the threat behind the words was clear. 'I've been lonely here since you married,' she went on. 'I would like the company.'

'In another couple of weeks,' Angela said, 'I may have some money myself.'

'Don't be ridiculous, dear. Whatever can you mean?'

Before Angela could answer there was a knock on the door and Margaret walked in nervously, carrying a tray.

'Thank you, Margaret,' said Mrs Mount, taking the tray from her, but the girl hovered in the doorway.

'Excuse me, Mrs Mount,' she said, 'but the nurse is doing Mrs Richardson's dressing and she can't find the bandages.'

'They're in the cupboard where they always are,' Mrs Mount said, implying that Margaret or the nurse, or both, were fools.

'I'm sorry,' Margaret said. 'They're not. They've all gone.'

'Can't you manage for a moment by yourselves!' Mrs Mount swept out to deal with the problem, her face still fixed in a smile.

Angela sipped weak tea and waited. Her mother was soon back, shaking her head at the extravagance of her staff.

'All gone,' she said. 'It's ridiculous. There were boxes in that cupboard at the beginning of the month. Now, where were we?'

'I was saying,' Angela said slowly, 'that I might not need to work here after all. I might be able to find the money to clear all my debts.'

'Where would you find that sort of money?' Mrs Mount demanded. But Angela could be stubborn too and refused to say.

Anything would be better than working here, she thought. Anything would be better than bed-sores and bandages and emptying commodes. Prison would be better than that. Harold should have given me the money when I asked him. He would have given it to me in the end. He shouldn't have been so mean.

'I'm sorry,' Angela said. 'I wouldn't be any good at this work. I'd let you down. I'm not as patient as you.'

It was as if she had bestowed sainthood on her mother. Mrs Mount beamed and simpered.

'You're a good girl,' she said. 'A very good girl. But if this money doesn't appear you won't have any choice.'

Chapter Four

The next day the school was closed, not as a mark of respect for Harold Medburn, but because the police needed more time there. Irene Hunt was asked to work as usual. She was deputy head and the Education Department at County Hall wanted her to be at the school, though there was little she could do. She would have preferred to be at home. It seemed unfair that she would not benefit from the additional holiday.

Miss Hunt liked to be at home. She lived in a small bungalow twenty miles north of Heppleburn on the coast. She had bought it the year before in preparation for her retirement. Everyone who saw it, and many who had never been near the place, said it was quite unsuitable for an elderly lady. It was build next to a farm at the top of a low cliff. The nearest village was two miles away at the end of a lane. She had views of Coquet Island, of ruined castles and bare hillsides, but it was cold and in a wind the draughts rattled under the doors, flapping rugs and curtains. Towards the sea there was an exposed garden, terraced and held back from the cliff by low stone walls. It was too big, her critics said, to be managed by one person. Miss Hunt had great plans for the garden. The bungalow suited her very well. For too long she had worried about what other people thought of her. Now for her last years she deserved to be allowed to live as she pleased.

Harold Medburn had been one of the fiercest opponents of her move from the convenient new house at Heppleburn to the bungalow on the cliff.

'It's too far away,' he had grumbled when she mentioned the

move one day in the staff room. 'You'll be late and in winter you'll never get here. You should think again about it.'

She had given up arguing with him years before and ignored him then. When finally she announced that the move had taken place he was astounded. He had been certain that she would take his advice.

Miss Hunt liked the bungalow because of its privacy. She had been entranced by the large windows and the clarity of the light. She had enjoyed painting in watercolour since she was a student and hoped with more time to develop her skill. She would be sensible, of course, about the house – it was no romantic dream. She would have double glazing fitted with the lump sum she received on her retirement. But she was quite passionate about the house. She was determined to end her days there on her own. If ever the time came when she was unable to look after herself, she would take her own life. She knew what it was like to be in another person's power and refused to contemplate that happening again, even if that power were the institutional kindness of a geriatric hospital or old people's home.

The police arrived at the bungalow to interview her on the Sunday morning, and early on the same afternoon Matthew came to see her.

He had woken early. It was still dark and he felt ill. He switched on the bedside lamp to see what time it was, but the sudden light hurt his head and he had to shut his eyes. When he opened them again, slowly, he saw his clothes scattered over the bedroom floor and an empty beer can propped on the window sill. He could not remember getting home. His memory of the evening before returned gradually, and with a growing horror he recalled what had happened. Perhaps he was still drunk, because he fell again into a heavy sleep and when he woke up it was light and the milkman was whistling along the pavement outside his window.

He got out of bed and felt sick again. Before dressing, before even making tea, he picked all the clothes from the bedroom floor and stuffed them into the washing machine in the kitchen. It was as if he wanted to clear away all traces of the previous evening.

He wanted to pretend that it had never happened. The washing machine was an old one of his mother's, a present when he had first moved to Heppleburn.

'I can go to the launderette,' he had said. 'I managed before.' A washing machine seemed a frightening symbol of domesticity.

'You're not a student now,' she said. 'Besides, I need a new one.'

His mother had been thrilled when he had been appointed to Heppleburn school. It had been her idea that he should apply. She had seen the advertisement in *The Teacher* and pointed it out to him. 'Northumberland,' she said, 'it's the most beautiful county in England. If you got that I could come up and stay with you in the holidays.' Now that seemed a long time ago.

As he remembered his mother, he thought he should write to her. He always wrote to her on Sunday mornings. It seemed important to maintain the usual routine, though he felt so ill. He made tea and toast and sat at the small table in the kitchen while the washing machine churned. He wrote: 'There was a Hallowe'en party at the school last night. I think everyone enjoyed it.' Except me, he thought. I didn't enjoy it at all.

He addressed the envelope and propped the letter on the mantelpiece, because he could not buy a stamp until the next day. I'll take it to school, he thought, and buy a stamp there. He decided to visit Miss Hunt on impulse, because he needed to be out of the house, because she had helped him at the party and because he wanted to find out how the evening had ended. He lived in a flat over a chemist's shop and his head thumped as he clattered down the concrete steps to the pavement.

Miss Hunt saw him coming from a long way off. She watched him leave the main road and cycle down the lane. It took him longer than it normally would have done, because he was cycling against the wind. She was ridiculously pleased to see him. She watched him from the bedroom window with the pair of binoculars she kept for looking at boats in the bay. His hair was blown away from his face. He was wearing old clothes – a navy jersey and denim jeans with a red patch on the knee. He looked much younger and happier than when he was teaching. Perhaps he would be happy more often now. When he rode into the farmyard, moving quickly because be was sheltered by the buildings from the pressure of the wind, she already had the bungalow door open to greet him. She was holding a black tom cat.

Matthew's face was red from the exertion of cycling. The farm dogs raced up to him, barking furiously, then started to jump up at him, so his jersey was muddy and even more disreputable than ever.

'Come in,' she said warmly.

She was as tall as he was. Her hair was short and well cut. She had style, he thought, despite her age. He propped his bicycle against the low wall which surrounded her front garden and followed her towards the house. The dogs bounced after him to the gate, still barking. His arms seemed very long and bony, bare wrists stretched out of the sleeves of his jersey. He sat on the door mat in the wood-frame porch and took off the suede desert boots with broken laces which she had never seen before. Then he walked into the house. He was wearing odd socks.

Irene Hunt felt very fond of him. He reminded her of the only man she had ever loved.

'I came to thank you,' he said, 'for making sure I got home last night. I'm afraid I made a fool of myself.'

She looked at him sharply.

'Haven't the police been to see you?' she asked.

He shook his head. 'I didn't do anything illegal did I?' he asked. 'I was very drunk. I can't remember everything, but I don't think anyone called the police. You persuaded me to leave before I made too much of a fool of myself.'

She was thrown by this. It had not occurred to her that he would not have heard that Medburn had been killed. He had left the party long before Robson found the headmaster's body in the small playground, but surely someone would have told him.

'The headmaster is dead,' she said, watching him closely. 'He was murdered. Robson found his body. At first we thought it was suicide but the police say that's impossible.'

He said nothing for a while. The colour drained from his face.

46

She led him into the kitchen and sat him on a rocking chair by the boiler. She made him tea.

'I could have killed him,' Matthew said. 'I was mad enough. He called me in to see him on Friday night. I'd never been to his home before. He was more friendly than he'd ever been and even offered me a drink. I didn't know what to expect.' He hesitated and then the words came out in a rush. 'He said I'd never make a teacher and he didn't think I should complete the probationary year. It would be more dignified, he said, to resign and if I wasn't prepared to do that he'd try to get me sacked.' He looked at her. 'I wanted to kill him.'

'Is that why you drank so much on Saturday night?'

He nodded. 'It didn't help,' he said. 'But I felt so helpless. Do the police know who killed him?'

'I don't know,' she said. 'They were here this morning, but it's impossible to tell what they're thinking. They were asking a lot of questions about his wife.'

She opened the kitchen door onto the paved area at the back of the house, to let out the black cat which had been moaning at her leg. She looked down over the terraced garden to the cliff edge. A salt breeze blew in and they might have been in the open air.

'I wouldn't kill him,' she said. 'I wouldn't jeopardize all this for that man. He wasn't worth it.'

She shut the door and the noise of the sea, which had invaded the kitchen, faded.

'I understand that the police have taken Kitty Medburn into custody for questioning,' Irene Hunt said suddenly. She was unsure how much she should tell Matthew, but it was comforting to have someone to talk to. 'Apparently he was having an affair with another woman. The police asked me if I knew anything about it.'

'Did you?'

'No,' she said. 'He was a very secretive man. Clever and very secretive. I don't blame Kitty for killing him. She's had a lot to put up with. I don't think anyone should be charged with his murder. We're better off without him.'

If Matthew was shocked by her bitterness he did not comment

on it. Perhaps he was more concerned by his own problems. He sat with his stockinged feet on the wooden rung of the rocking chair, his hands cupped around the mug of tea.

'What should I do about the teaching?' he asked abruptly.

'What do you mean?' she said.

'Should I carry on with it?'

'Of course you should,' she said briskly, a teacher to her fingertips, urging a favourite child to have confidence in his own ability. 'With a bit of support you'll make an excellent teacher. Forget that the meeting with Medburn ever happened. There's no need to tell the police about it. It's no business of theirs, after all.'

Then she insisted on taking him for a walk along the cliff. Spikes of sunshine pierced the cloud, but it was still very cold. She pointed out her favourite features of the landscape and enjoyed his admiration of the view. Inland there was a subsidence lake, backed by a new conifer plantation. A skein of geese flew overhead, calling, then landed on the water. At the bottom of the cliff a girl on a chestnut horse galloped along the sandy beach, splashing through the pools. The drops of water glistened in the sunlight.

'It's lovely,' he said. He had never been to her house before. 'This is just the sort of house I'd live in. But don't you find it lonely?'

'No,' she said. 'I get on well with my neighbour. She's rather confused and eccentric at times, but we've become good friends. Her sons farm the land and live in a bungalow in the village. She doesn't want to leave the house. I don't blame her.'

Back in the house she made more tea and toast. There was a fire in the living room and she refused to put on the light. Then she might feel she should draw the curtains and shut out the sea. The room was hung with her paintings.

It was nearly dusk when he set off on his bike for his flat in Heppleburn. She had not wanted him to go. It had been one of the most pleasant afternoons Irene Hunt could remember and she felt relaxed and ready to return to school the next day. She had long ago given up any thought of a family life and had persuaded herself that she would not enjoy it anyway, but this afternoon she regretted that she had never married. When Matthew left she felt very alone.

She got to school at a quarter to nine on the Monday morning. The police were on the premises. There was still white tape around the small playground and a uniformed constable stood by the wooden door in the wall. She ignored the activity and went straight to her classroom, as she would have done if the children had been there. At the main door into the school a policeman stopped her and asked who she was, then let her through. To Miss Hunt the police were an anonymous body, like Her Majesty's Inspectorate of Education or the Inland Revenue. She supposed that the men on their hands and knees in the playground had some specialized function, but she had no real interest. As her retirement came closer she was coming to feel that she was a stranger in the school. She was increasingly more detached from everything that went on there, even the horror of murder. She longed for her time as a teacher to be over, so she could spend her days in her bungalow with her paint and her cat and the noise of the waves.

At half past twelve when the children would usually have gone out to play before lunch she went to the staff room and made a cup of coffee. It was a luxury to have the place to herself. It was strangely tidy and uncluttered. She wondered if she should offer to make drinks for the policemen in the hall but decided not to disturb them. They might think she was prying like a common gossip. The kettle was just starting to boil when there was a knock on the door and a plain-clothed policeman came in, stooping slightly as if the door was too low. She recognized the inspector who had come to her bungalow the day before.

Ramsay had been at the school since early morning. After his wife had left him there was nothing to keep him at home and he was aware of the comments of his colleagues. Just because he couldn't keep his wife, they said, he seems to think none of us want to spend time with our families. They said that he'd lost his sense of proportion, that there was more to life than work, after all. To Ramsay there was little more to life than work.

He had insisted that Medburn's office, the staff room and all the corridors should be fingerprinted. When they told him it would take days, he shrugged. The murderer must have come into the school, he said, to get the black gown. No one had said that a long murder investigation was easy. Usually you found the culprit in the first hour. If not it was hard work. So he expected them to work hard. They knew who had killed Harold Medburn. They had to prove it.

He waited to talk to Miss Hunt until he saw her go into the staff room. He thought she might be more prepared to give him her full attention there than in the classroom where there was work to do.

'Would you like coffee?' she asked. When he had come to the bungalow the day before he had pleased her. 'I'm making some for myself.'

'That would be very nice,' he said. He seemed relaxed and easy. He sat on one of the chairs without being asked.

'Now,' she said, 'How can I help you, Inspector?' He was tall and dark and quite athletic, with a gentle local accent. She had known physical education teachers of a similar type. He was middle-aged but fit and wearing well. She could imagine him rock climbing.

'Have you time to answer some questions?' he asked. 'It would save me having to trouble you at home again.'

'Of course,' she said.

'The gown he was wearing when the body was found,' Ramsay said. 'It *was* his?'

'Oh yes,' she said, and despite herself there was a trace of bitterness in her voice. 'He never went to university as a young man, you know. He wasn't particularly academic. He went to college later, in middle age, and took a Bachelor of Education then. We all thought he intended to try for promotion to a bigger school, but he never moved. He was very proud of his gown.'

'Where was it kept?'

'In his office. On a hook on the door.'

'I see,' he said. He took a pipe from his pocket and began to fill it with tobacco from a leather pouch. She waited for him to light it, but he seemed to change his mind and laid it carefully on the low table before him.

'How did Mr Medburn die?' Irene asked. She was enjoying Ramsay's company. The question came naturally.

'He was dead before he was hung up,' the policeman said. 'He was strangled but not by the noose of bandages. We think he may have been drugged first.'

They drank instant coffee in silence.

'Is there anything else you want to ask me?' she said in the end. 'I think I should go back to my classroom. I feel I should be working even though the children aren't here.'

'Did he take any private pupils?' Ramsay asked.

'No,' she said. 'I'm sure not.'

'He didn't work for one of the examination boards, marking papers?'

'No,' she said. 'He was a primary specialist.'

'So he had no other income?'

'I'm sure he didn't.'

'No one seems very sorry he's dead,' the policeman said suddenly, and she thought perhaps he was clever, more imaginative than she had first supposed.

'No,' she said. 'He wasn't very popular.'

'Why was that then? Did he pick on the children?'

'Not on the children, no. He was a good teacher in a lot of ways, though a little boring by today's standards. No. Adults were his victims.'

'Did he knock his wife around?' He asked the question in the same level, matter-of-fact tone.

She was very shocked. She supposed that in his work the detective must mix often with men who beat their wives, but it seemed offensive to suggest that she was acquainted with such people. 'No,' she said. 'There was nothing like that.' Then, feeling surprisingly disloyal, she added: 'He was too subtle, you see, for that kind of violence.'

'You sound almost glad that he's dead,' Ramsay said.

Irene Hunt thought then that her original assessment of him was correct but that after all he had an instinctive intelligence, like an animal's.

'Do I?' she said. 'Life will be a lot easier, you know, without him.'

She took their cups to the sink and washed them. The policeman sat back in his chair and watched her.

Outside in the corridor, Jack Robson was cleaning the floor where the police had finished. He had heard every word of the conversation, but neither the policeman nor Miss Hunt took any notice of him. He was as much a part of the school furniture as the blackboards and the wall bars in the gym.

All day, in the village, Jack had been asking questions about Medburn and Angela Brayshaw. Patty's description of her conversation with Angela had excited him. There was already the possibility of another motive.

Perhaps Medburn had another lover. Perhaps there were other jealousies. Perhaps Angela had found Medburn's attentions unwelcome, hateful even. Jack was sure that someone in Heppleburn would have information about Medburn, and that morning he set out to make it known that he needed the information too. First he went to the small chemist shop in the high street to ask if someone had been in during the previous week to buy a quantity of bandages. The police had been there before him but it gave him the opportunity to explain why he wanted to know. Medburn's murderer must have had bandages, he said, to twist into a noose. He made a nuisance of himself in the grocer's shop and the post office, where he waited to talk to the pensioners, because they were always the best gossips. They all knew him as a diligent and caring councillor who fought with officials and bureaucrats on their behalf. They wanted to help him. By lunch-time, when he had to go to school, everyone in the village knew he intended to prove Kitty innocent. Everyone in Heppleburn knew where to find him. He had thought that all he had to do was wait for the information to come to him. Now, Ramsay's questions to Irene Hunt about the headmaster suggested that he had a source of income they had been unable to trace. Medburn was mean. His reluctance to part with money was legendary in the village and Jack would not have been surprised to learn that he had some other work, something the taxman knew nothing about. If he could discover what that was, he might find another candidate for murder. He had other questions to put in the village.

He stayed in the school until five thirty and by then most of the policemen had gone, and it was ready for classes to resume the next day. He took off his brown overall, hung it in his room and lit a cigarette. As he walked down the corridor to go out into the playground, the inspector who had been talking to Irene Hunt waved at him through the window of the hall. Jack thought Ramsay's face was familiar and he wondered if perhaps he had worked down the pit with the policeman's father.

Outside it was nearly dark and he could see the orange street lights, filtered through hazy smoke, in the village below him. The sudden cold weather had encouraged people to light fires, and a cloud of smoke hung in the valley.

As he walked down the steep lane the familiar smell of the smoke and sulphur took him back to childhood. It was the smell of winter. It reminded him of the back kitchen at home, where his mother made pans of leek broth on the black-leaded range and boiled kettles of hot water for his father's bath.

There was a fire in the bar of the Northumberland Arms. It was a gloomy place with dark-stained wood panelling and leaded windows. The lights never seemed quite bright enough. During the war the pub had been used by submariners stationed in Blyth and the walls were hung with photographs of men in uniform and ships and submarines. The pub had just opened and the bar was empty. The landlady, a thin, grey little woman with twig-like arms and enormous energy, was putting clean ashtrays on the tables and seemed surprised to see him.

'By man, you're early tonight,' she said.

'I need a drink,' he said. 'I've worked hard today getting the school ready for the bairns to go back.'

'Are the police still there then?' she asked. She was avid for news. He hoped she had other information with which to reciprocate.

'Aye, I don't know when they'll be finished. They say that the school can open again tomorrow. Miss Hunt will be in charge until they get a new head.'

She polished the last ashtray with a duster then scuttled behind the bar to serve him.

'A pint of Scotch is it?'

He nodded and watched her pull the beer. 'And something for yourself,' he said.

She poured a small glass of whisky and sipped at it, like a pigeon taking grain.

'What do you think of Mr Medburn getting himself murdered?' she asked. Nothing so exciting had ever happened in the village before.

'I don't think Kitty killed him,' he said firmly.

'Do you not?' Her eyes were bright and she pecked again at the whisky.

'No.' He looked at her across the bar. 'You haven't heard anything,' he said, 'which might help? People talk to you.'

'Folks were scared of him,' she said. 'I know that.'

'What do you mean?'

'You should talk to Miss Hunt,' she said. 'She was scared of him. My daughter was dinner nanny at the school years ago and she heard some things then . . .'

'What sort of things?'

But she refused to say and changed the subject abruptly.

'I've heard Angela Brayshaw got herself into a terrible lot of debt,' she said. 'They were going to take her house off her, but her mother stepped in and paid off the building society. I hear Angela will be working at the nursing home now. She won't like that.'

He drank the rest of his beer. 'No,' he said, 'she won't like that.' He smiled broadly. 'Thanks,' he said, 'you've been a great help.'

She winked at him as he went out. Walking out of the gloomy pub into the street he almost bumped into the policeman who had been at the school. It occurred to him that Ramsay had followed him and was waiting for him. As if I was a bloody criminal, he thought. He had never liked the police, and the miners' strike had made things worse.

'Councillor Robson,' Ramsay said. 'I was hoping to talk to you.'

'I can't stop now,' Robson said. 'My daughter's expecting me.' It was a lie. He had made no arrangements to visit Patty.

'I'll give you a lift,' Ramsay said smoothly. 'I was wanting to talk to Mrs Atkins again.'

'You'll be lucky if you get any sense out of her tonight,' Jack said spitefully. 'It'll be chaos in there. It always is. The bairns'll not be in bed yet.'

'All the same,' Ramsay said, 'you'll not say no to a lift.'

His car was parked outside the British Legion Hall.

'You seem to have been taking a lot of interest in this case,' the inspector said.

Jack remained stubbornly silent.

'If you have any information you will come to see me,' Ramsay said gently. 'I understand that Mrs Medburn was an old friend of yours.'

Sly bastard, Jack thought. What business is it of yours? You think she killed him. But still he said nothing. He allowed himself to be helped into the big, comfortable car, then Ramsay drove to Patty's house and parked immaculately close to the kerb.

'Surely you don't need to come in now,' Jack said irritably. 'You can talk to Patty tomorrow.'

'I'll just come to the door,' Ramsay said, 'and ask Mrs Atkins if it's convenient.'

Jack had hoped that it would be a mess, that Ramsay would find it impossible to make himself heard above the noise of the television and the children's games. He had thought that they would still be at their tea, had imagined the smell of fried food, the floor covered with Andrew's Lego and Jennifer's crayons. But Patty was alone there. Jim had taken Andrew to cubs and Jennifer was at a friend's for tea. The toys had been put away and the dishes, if unwashed, were hidden in the kitchen.

'Dad,' she said as she opened the door and saw him standing

there, a Charlie Chaplin figure with the policeman by his side. 'What have you been doing? Why are you here?'

'I thought Mr Robson was expected,' Ramsay said in mock surprise. She was aware of him immediately, felt flushed and awkward in front of him as she invited him in, moved a pile of magazines from a chair so that Ramsay could sit down.

'It was kind of you to bring my father home,' she said.

Look at her! Jack thought. Just because he's got a pretty face.

'It was no trouble,' the policeman said. 'I was hoping you could help me again. It's about Harold Medburn. No one seems to have known him very well.'

'I'll help you if I can,' she said, despite Jack's obvious disapproval, 'but I only ever met him at school. Dad probably knew him better than me.'

'I'm interested in the sort of man he was,' Ramsay continued. 'Were people frightened of him?'

'He wasn't liked,' Patty said. 'I suppose we all found him a bit . . . intimidating. What do you think, Dad?'

But Jack did not answer. Ramsay's question to Irene Hunt and to Patty had suddenly taken on a new significance. He remembered what the landlady of the Northumberland Arms had said.

'Why do you want to know? he asked, turning suddenly towards the policeman.

Ramsay shrugged. 'We're just trying to tie up some loose ends,' he said.

But Jack did not believe him. Medburn was a blackmailer, he thought. That's what it's all about. He had money they can't explain away. And I know who he was blackmailing.

When he went with Patty to show Ramsay to the door he was almost gracious and thanked him for the lift.

Ramsay hesitated for a moment outside the door. He liked Robson. The old man reminded him of his father. But Ramsay was convinced that Kitty Medburn had murdered her husband and thought the old man was playing foolish games.

Chapter Five

Patty persuaded Jack to spend the night with her and the family – his house would be cold, she said – but he found it hard to sleep and wished he had insisted on going home. First he was disturbed by Jennifer who refused to settle on the camp bed in her parents' room; and when the house was quiet he thought of Kitty and the tall policeman and the people who had been Medburn's victims. They'd be glad that Medburn was dead and would want to forget him. Jack had started the investigation with his intentions firm and starkly clear. He would save Kitty whatever the cost in reputation or inconvenience to other people. Now it seemed the thing was not so simple. If Kitty were innocent someone else must be guilty, and the unpleasantness which had surrounded Medburn during his life would continue long after he had been buried. Jack would need to discover Medburn's secrets and would become as much an object of hatred as the headmaster had been. Yet as he lay in Jennifer's small bed waiting for the morning a childish persistence and romanticism made him cling to his original purpose. He saw Kitty as Rapunzel, locked in a tower, and himself as the prince charged to rescue her. Then, as in the stories, they would live happily ever after.

He read until three and fell into a tense and fitful sleep. When he woke several hours later Andrew was practising the recorder and Jennifer was screaming that she must wear the pink jumper with the Care Bears on it, even if it meant disturbing Grandpa to fetch it. Patty brought him tea and told him to stay where he was, but he got up.

He preferred to be at work, where it was quieter.

'But I need to talk to you,' Patty said. She was burning toast. Upstairs on the landing Jim was cursing because Andrew was playing the recorder in the bathroom and he wanted to shave.

'What were you doing in the village yesterday bothering everyone?' she asked. 'People are saying you're mad.'

Jack pretended not to hear. 'I have to go,' he said. 'I'll have to unlock the school to let them all in.'

'But what do you want me to do?' she asked.

Jack thought. 'Talk to the vicar,' he said. 'He knew Medburn as well as anyone. He was always in the church. Will you do that?'

She nodded and scraped flakes of charcoal from the toast into the stainless steel sink.

'Take care,' she said, looking round with concern at his exhausted face. 'When can I see you?'

'This afternoon,' he said. 'I'll be home this afternoon. You can talk to me then.'

It was the first severe frost of the autumn and in the street men were scraping ice off precious cars. Everywhere was as white as if snow had fallen and as he walked briskly along the pavement his breath came in clouds of steam. The fallen leaves which had collected water in the gutters had frozen, so they crunched as he crossed the road, and made his way into the village. He called to everyone he knew, hoping that one of them would have information about Medburn's death, information which would lead to Kitty's release. Outside the Northumberland Arms he paused to chat to the lollipop lady who was retrieving her sign from one of the pub's out-houses. She stood on the edge of the pavement stamping white boots, blowing hot air into gloved hands and waiting for her first customer.

'Back to work again today,' he said. He hovered there, waiting for someone to approach him. 'You could have stayed in bed yesterday.'

'Aye,' she said. 'I could have done. But no one bothered to tell us and I stood here for an hour wondering what had happened to the bairns.'

They laughed together and he crossed the main road away from the pub and walked up the lane towards the school. The playground was empty. He had half expected the police to be there and it was a relief. He unlocked the doors and carried crates of milk into the kitchen, then went to his room. He filled his kettle at the sink in the boys' toilet and plugged it in. While he was waiting for it to boil he lit a cigarette. It was the same ritual he followed every morning, yet it was not the same. Everything he did seemed sharper, more urgent, more exciting. He had expected to slip gently into retirement and eventually into death. The challenge of discovering who had killed Harold Medburn was new, and he was enjoying it.

He sat with his tea by the small window and watched the teachers arrive. Miss Hunt came first, driving a red Metro. She was wearing black boots and a black woollen cape and reminded him of the pictures of witches which had been pinned to the walls of the classrooms on Hallowe'en. Immediately afterwards Matthew Carpenter walked in through the gate from the lane. He was dressed in a green parka with the hood pulled over his head, so he looked like a teenager. The teachers shouted to each other. It was something meaningless about the weather, but Jack thought they would never have done that if Medburn had been there. Then each would have scuttled into their own classroom without a word, afraid of attracting attention or censure. Everyone, it seemed, felt a sense of release after Medburn's death.

On his way to his classroom Matthew called into Jack's room. 'Will you be going to the post later for Miss Hunt?' he asked. Jack nodded. 'Could you take this letter for my mum? I wrote it on Sunday and forgot to post it.'

Jack nodded once more and wondered again that such a normal conversation was possible.

Children began to run into the playground, followed by scolding mothers with toddlers in pushchairs. The girls formed circles, sang 'Brown girl in the ring' and 'In and out the dusty bluebells' until they were red with exertion and the circles dissolved and reformed with new members. The boys fought and tried to slide on the frosty concrete. All the children were noisy and excitable.

Patty arrived in a rush, her shaggy hair looking as if it had never seen a brush, the trousers of her tracksuit splashed with paint. She kissed the children and walked away in the direction of the vicarage. As she went she passed Paul Wilcox. He stopped her and talked so intently that he did not notice his daughter climbing out of the buggy to play with the other children until his son tugged his sleeve and pointed out her naughtiness. Jack wondered what the man was saying, and waited. Angela Brayshaw came late, holding her daughter's hand, but not late enough to avoid the other mothers, the stares, the whispers. They had all heard the rumours Jack had spread in the village the day before.

Paul Wilcox turned away from Patty and began to walk towards the school. At first, of course, Medburn's death had come as a great relief to him. There would be no need now to admit to Hannah that he had been unfaithful. They could work out their family problems without that pressure. There would be no more of the frightening phone calls which summoned him to come to the school, just to discuss a question of Parents' Association policy, and were an excuse for Medburn to scare him. He arrived on those afternoons at Medburn's office white and shaking. Medburn would lecture him on morality and virtue, then ask for money. Every time he was summoned Wilcox swore to himself that this time he would not pay, and on each occasion the demand for payment came almost as a relief because it meant that the interview was over. He was sorry when Kitty was arrested – he had nothing against Medburn's wife – but he had himself to think of first.

On the Saturday night, after the body had been discovered he had been calm. He and Hannah had drunk tea and discussed the murder.

'What an extraordinary thing to have happened!' Hannah said, her eyes big. 'Whoever would want to kill a village headmaster?'

He had agreed with her. It was extraordinary, he said.

He had slept deeply and well. Then on the Sunday morning they learned that Kitty Medburn had been arrested and he thought the whole thing would be over.

He had begun to be troubled by the idea of the letters before he heard that Jack Robson had been going round the village asking questions, claiming that Kitty Medburn was innocent, insinuating that Angela Brayshaw was somehow involved. He should have thought before about the letters. He tried to persuade himself that they would have no significance for anyone else, but he could not forget them and by the time Mrs Irving, the cleaning lady, arrived on Monday afternoon he was tense and jumpy.

He never usually minded her gossip. It was a change to have someone else to talk to. But that afternoon it was all about the murder and the fuss Jack Robson was making in the village.

'But what can he possibly know about it?' Paul had demanded, and realized at once that he must sound too aggressive.

'He says he knows more than the police,' Mrs Irving replied. 'He's a canny man, Councillor Robson.'

'What nonsense.'

But as he thought about it Paul Wilcox thought that perhaps Jack Robson *did* know more than the police. After all he worked in the school. He would have access to Medburn's office, perhaps even to the headmaster's desk. There was no knowing what he might have overheard. The thought obsessed him and he could not stop brooding on it. When she came home that evening Hannah could tell that he was upset, and was sympathetic.

'It'll be delayed shock,' she said. 'You worked with Mr Medburn. You were close to him. It's natural that you should feel like this.'

He wanted to tell her that her sympathy was misguided, that he did not deserve it, but he was too weak and frightened.

By Tuesday morning he was determined to find out how much Jack Robson knew. He could not bear the anxiety of this uncertainty. He tried to talk to Patty in the playground, but she seemed to know nothing, so when the school bell went and the playground was empty of parents and children he went to look for the caretaker.

He found Jack Robson in his room. He realized that Jack had seen him coming and was expecting him. He had left Lizzie strapped in her buggy in the playground, with a bag of sweeties to keep her quiet.

'Come in, man,' Jack Robson said when he tapped on the door. 'What can I do for you?'

Wilcox did not know what to say. He stood on the threshold and his mind went blank. He started to stammer some excuse but Jack interrupted him.

'You'll have come about Harold Medburn,' he said.

Wilcox was the last person Jack had expected to see. Surely his set were beyond Medburn's power. He came from the south, he was wealthy, the chairman of the Parents' Association. If anything Medburn should have been in awe of him. Yet here he stood, gawping like a goldfish. Jack looked at him with interest.

'You'll have come about Harold Medburn,' he repeated, then taking pity on the man he added: 'I expect you want to know why I'm so interested in the case.'

'Yes,' Wilcox said gratefully, 'that's right.' He composed himself. 'We must think about the reputation of the school,' he said. 'We don't want any more adverse publicity than is strictly necessary. You're a governor, you'll understand that.'

'And we don't want an innocent woman to go to gaol,' Jack said quickly.

There was a pause.

'Do you think Kitty Medburn is innocent?' Wilcox asked.

'Aye.'

'What makes you think that?'

'What makes you so interested?'

'I've told you,' Wilcox blustered. 'I'm concerned about the school. We want the thing over quickly.'

'Kitty Medburn is a friend of mine,' Jack said. 'I don't think she could have killed him.'

Is that all? Wilcox thought, overwhelmed with relief. He doesn't know about the letters, he has no evidence at all. He's just a romantic fool.

Jack Robson recognized the relief and wished he had not given so much away.

'Can I ask you some questions?' he said. 'As you're here.'

'Of course.' There was nothing to be frightened of now.

'You used to come to the school quite often,' Jack said. 'What did you and Medburn have to talk about?'

'Oh,' Wilcox said. 'General matters concerning the school. Mr Medburn was interested in getting feedback from the parents.'

That, Jack thought, was a fantasy. Medburn hadn't given a shit what the parents thought.

But Wilcox was continuing: 'If you're looking for another suspect for Mr Medburn's murder, perhaps you should talk to young Matthew Carpenter. Did you know that the headmaster was determined to get rid of him? Mr Medburn was going to try to persuade him to resign and if that didn't work he was going to sack him. The headmaster asked me what the parents thought of Mr Carpenter's teaching.'

'That's why you came to the school last week?'

'That, and to discuss the final arrangements for the Hallowe'en party with Miss Hunt.'

He stood up and held out his hand to Jack. He saw with satisfaction that it was steady and unshaking.

'I'll have to go now,' he said, 'my daughter's waiting outside.'

In the playground he took a deep breath. It was unfortunate, he thought, that he should have shifted suspicion onto young Matthew Carpenter, but he must think of his own safety. He thought he had handled things rather well. It was only later in the day that his anxiety about the letters returned and he decided that something had to be done about them.

Jack Robson watched Wilcox from the window. The information about Matthew Carpenter had been interesting, but he thought he had learned more about Wilcox himself. The man was frightened. In the school hall the children began to sing 'All things bright and beautiful'.

The vicarage was big and ugly and had seen better days. It had been built a hundred years before at the same time as the church to serve the expanding community, though few of the men who worked in the pit worshipped there. They went every Sunday to the Methodist chapel in the village. In the churchyard were the graves of men who had lost their lives in the colliery accidents, and by drowning, and of women who had died in childbirth. Only recently, it seemed, had it become common to die of old age.

Patty walked past the tombstones on her way to the house. Brown chrysanthemums, covered in frost, lay on her mother's grave. She wondered, briefly, where Medburn would be buried. Here, she presumed, as he was such a pillar of the church. It was a high, exposed place. The trees around the church were bent and some were bare, stripped of their leaves by the wind the previous day. As she walked along the icy path to the vicarage she noticed that there were blackbirds everywhere and that the clear air was full of their song.

She saw the vicar through his study window before she rang the bell. He was running the pages of the parish magazine off a primitive printing machine. His fingers were stained with blue ink and he turned the handle with great ferocity. He was red and flushed although there seemed to be no heating in the vicarage. Before becoming a clergyman he had been in the merchant navy, though now he seemed too thin, too quiet, too academic for a sailor. He looked to Patty no older than when he had come to Heppleburn ten years before. He was probably in his mid-forties. His arrival at the church from the south of England had coincided with a period of religious enthusiasm in her life. Perhaps he had been the cause of it. She had attended regularly, had even, for one disastrous winter, been in the choir. Like all her interests it had passed and now she only came to church when the children had some special Sunday school activity and for the Midnight Communion of Christmas Eve.

Peter Mansfield, the vicar, seemed to feel a personal responsibility for her disaffection. He seemed to regard each attendance as a possible rebirth of faith, would speak to her specially as she left the church, saying that he hoped to see her again soon. Each time he was disappointed. Now, when he let her into the draughty hall he greeted her with great affection and she felt a fraud as if she were there on false pretences.

'How good to see you!' he said. 'Come in. Shall I take your coat? Or would you rather keep it on for a while.'

'I'll keep it,' she said.

In the cavernous corners of the house there were competing noises and strange echoes. His wife was a music teacher and must have had an early pupil because the nerve-jangling squeal of a poorly played violin came from a room at the end of the corridor. Upstairs there was the surprising sound of a pop record.

They had taken in a lodger, the vicar said in explanation, an unmarried mother whose parents had thrown her out. As if on cue a baby started crying. He seemed to take it all for granted but to Patty the sounds were tantalizing, glimpses of a freer, more confident way of living. She wished she knew more about the household. Like the family in the old mill it had a sophistication she associated with the south.

'Come in,' Peter said again, taking Patty's arm and leading her into his study. He must have seen that she was cold because he stooped and lit a small Calor gas heater.

'Now,' he said. 'How can I help you?'

'It's about Harold Medburn,' she said, then stopped. She was not sure how to continue. But there had always been an element of hero worship in her relationship with Mansfield and she decided that she could trust him with the truth. 'My father doesn't think that Kitty killed him,' she said in a rush. 'He wants to prove her innocent. He asked me to talk to you. Mr Medburn was a church warden and you must have known him very well.'

'I see.' He seemed surprised. He bent and warmed long, blue fingers in front of the fire to give himself time to think.

'Perhaps you think we shouldn't interfere,' she said.

'Not exactly,' he said. 'Don't you think it might be a little dangerous? It's not a thing to be taken lightly.'

'We're not taking it lightly,' she said. Then more honestly she added: 'Well, perhaps I am. I think it's exciting: It's hard to be sorry that Mr Medburn's dead. But Dad's not playing at this. Kitty was a friend of his a long time ago, before he met my mother. I've never seen him so serious about anything.'

'I don't understand how I can help,' Peter Mansfield said. 'I don't think Kitty killed her husband but I've no way of proving it.'

'You could tell us about Harold Medburn,' she said. 'He didn't have any other close friends. There's no one else to ask.'

'He was no friend of mine,' the vicar said so sharply that Patty gazed at him in astonishment. He looked awkward. Usually he wore kindness and tolerance as part of his clerical garb. 'I'm sorry,' he said. 'I didn't mean to be abrupt. I could never like Medburn. He made life very difficult for Julie and me when we first came. He was always prying and challenging my authority. He made Julie's life a misery. This was my first parish and I was too inexperienced to know how to deal with him. He undermined my confidence. At one time I thought I might have to leave the Church altogether.'

'But you didn't?'

'No,' Mansfield said. 'I suppose I realized what a sad little man he was. He was no threat to anyone.'

'Someone saw him as a threat,' Patty said. 'Someone killed him.'

'Yes,' Mansfield said earnestly, 'and that's why I find it hard to believe that the murderer is Kitty. She knew him too. She knew how weak and lonely he was. I don't think she was ever frightened of him – he could do nothing more to hurt her.'

'Why did they marry?' Patty asked. 'Did you ever find out?'

The vicar shook his head. 'That was long before my time and I never asked. Kitty has never come to church. Perhaps they were lonely. They both seem to be outsiders. Kitty does marvellous work with the old people in the village and everyone admires her, but she had no real friends.'

'Except my father,' Patty said.

'Perhaps,' the vicar said. He paused. 'I don't mean to be impertinent but I'm not sure how real that friendship is. You know Jack better than me but wasn't it a romantic memory that only returned when your father was on his own and Kitty was in trouble? I doubt whether the relationship would have survived years of marriage. She's a destructive woman in many ways.'

Patty did not know what to say. She assumed the vicar thought she might be hurt because Jack's affection was directed at someone other than her mother. She wanted to tell him that he was wrong, that she only wanted Jack to be happy.

'It matters a lot to him,' she said, 'to prove that Kitty's innocent.'

'Yes,' he said. 'I think it would be wiser to leave it to the police, but I can see that.'

'Is there nothing you can tell us which would help?' she asked.

'Medburn enjoyed power,' Mansfield said. 'It was an indication, I suppose, of his own inadequacy, but it was hard to be charitable about its consequences.'

'Was he evil?' she asked suddenly. It was a religious question. She might have been at confirmation class, though she would never have asked such a question of the old priest.

Mansfield seemed shocked and avoided a direct answer. 'That sort of judgement is not for me to make,' he said. He moved away from the fire and leant on the edge of his desk. He seemed to have come to a decision to talk to her. 'I remember soon after I came here,' he said, 'a woman came into the church. She was trying to trace Irene Hunt. That seemed a matter of great importance to her. Harold was in the church at the time and I suggested that she talk to him. I didn't know Medburn very well then, and although I was aware that Miss Hunt taught in the school I knew nothing about her. I can remember how pleased he was when I introduced the woman to him and I saw him again when she had gone. He was very smug and satisfied with himself. "What will Miss Hunt say," he said, "when I tell her?" When I knew him better I realized that I had probably given him the opportunity of discovering something about one of his staff, something which she would probably prefer him not to know. I felt as if I had betrayed a confidence.'

'Who was the woman?'

The vicar shook his head. 'I never asked,' he said. 'It was none of my business. But I expect that Harold found out all about her. I had the thing on my conscience for a long time afterwards. I never liked to ask Miss Hunt what came of it. Of course it's possible that I misjudged Harold and he simply passed on the address.'

'What was the woman like?' Patty asked.

'She was in her thirties,' he said. 'Tall and very dark. She caught my attention because she was remarkably beautiful.'

'Have you any idea who killed him?' she asked suddenly.

He hesitated before replying: 'No,' he said. 'I'm sorry.'

She was not sure he would tell her anyway.

'I think I should go now,' Patty said. She felt awkward again, sitting there, presuming to take his time. It was too easy to take him for granted and perhaps he resented her assumption that he was prepared to talk to her. She felt that he would want something in return – an indication that she might share his faith and commitment – and that she was unwilling to give.

He must have realized that, because he smiled sadly as he let her out into the garden and he said nothing about hoping to see her in church again. He seemed almost pleased to be rid of her. As she walked away from the house she heard the sound of the printing machine thumping again, and of someone playing a scale on the violin.

By the time she walked to her father's home the sun had melted the frost and the people she met in the street said what a beautiful day it was and that they must make the most of it before the winter came.

In the house nothing had changed since Joan had died, and very little was different from when she was a child. She opened the door with her own key and she might have been coming home after a day at school. There was the same red carpet with the pattern of flowers and leaves, the same hideous three-piece suite. The mantelshelf was crammed with the ornaments Joan had collected on her coach trips with the Mothers' Union. There was even the same smell of furniture polish. Patty went in to clean for Jack once a week and took far more care than she did with her own housework. Otherwise he managed for himself, much better than she would ever have imagined. Before Joan's death he had done nothing in the house. She had polished his boots, brought in the coal and added sugar to his tea. Now he cooked for himself and did his own laundry.

He was sitting in the front room by the fire, his boots off, reading a library book. Joan had liked the television but now he never watched it during the day. Patty offered to make some tea, but he put down his book and went into the kitchen to do it himself. He came back with the pot and cups on a tray and a packet of his favourite shortcake biscuits.

'Did you go to see the vicar?' he asked. She nodded and told the story of the mysterious woman who had come to the church looking for Irene Hunt.

'What do you make of it?' she asked.

'I think Medburn was blackmailing Miss Hunt,' he said. He remembered again what the landlady of the Northumberland Arms had said about the staff being frightened of the headmaster. His idea had been confirmed.

'Will you talk to her?' Patty said. 'Miss Hunt still makes me feel like a six-year-old.'

'I'll talk to her,' Jack said, 'but not in school. She'll give nothing away there. I'll wait until the weekend and go to see her at home.' He did not like to admit that he too was frightened of her.

'What do you make of Paul Wilcox?' he asked.

She shrugged. 'He's pleasant enough,' she said. 'A bit of a wimp.'

'He's scared of something,' Jack said. 'He came to see me today to find out how much I know.'

'He's no murderer,' she said. 'He'd not have the guts.'

'It must have been one of the Parents' Association or the staff,' he said. 'Someone with access to the school. No one else could have taken Medburn's gown from his room.'

'So it was one of us,' she said. She felt a sudden thrill of fear.

They drank their tea in silence. Patty would have liked to ask him about Kitty, about how he met her and how close they were, but she said nothing about Mansfield's theory that Jack's memory of Kitty Medburn was flawed – romanticized, distorted by his own loneliness. She was too excited by the investigation to want him to call it off now. Besides, he would never have believed her.

Chapter Six

Every day the local newspapers were full of the news of Medburn's murder and it was from the newspaper that Jack learned Kitty had been to court. There was even a film of her on the early evening television news, huddled among a crowd of policemen with a coat over her head, but he was too upset then to listen to the commentary. From the newspaper he learned that she had been charged with murder and remanded in custody to await trial. He was distressed by the news, by the huge headlines which talked about the WITCHES' NIGHT MURDER and which encouraged the readers to speculate that Kitty must have killed her husband by supernatural means. The media had been given no details of the method and circumstances of the murder, and the scarcity of information had led journalists into the realms of horror fiction. Jack would have liked to be in the court to give her comfort, so that she would have seen at least one friendly face, but despite his new experience in the council chamber he felt he was excluded completely from the criminal justice process. He did not know even if he would have been allowed to attend. He did not understand the terms used in the newspaper report. Was a remand centre the same as a prison? What did it mean that no plea was taken? He felt he was no use to her. She was being damned as a witch and there was nothing he could do.

It was a week after Harold Medburn's death, and he caught a bus to see Irene Hunt. Patty offered to drive him in the car but he decided to go alone. The conversation with Miss Hunt would need tact and Patty had precious little of that. The weather was still clear and sunny, but it was cold and the days were so short now that it was dark by late afternoon. He did not warn Miss Hunt of his visit. If she were not there he would wait for her. The newspaper reports of Kitty's ordeal had given him a sort of desperation.

The bus dropped him at Nellington, a small village with a pub and several houses and the grey scars of an open-cast mine. It was two o'clock when he climbed off the bus and he was tempted to go into the pub for a drink before he approached her, but he decided against it and began the walk down the lane to the bungalow.

Irene Hunt saw him coming – he was a slight, upright figure in a macintosh which was too long for him – and recognized him at once. She thought at first he was there to tell her that Matthew Carpenter had got himself into another scrape, then realized that was ridiculous. She was irritated by the unwanted company. If there was some problem at school, why had the man not phoned? She had thought the bungalow was secluded enough to protect her from this kind of intrusion. She did not want to appear too welcoming, and waited until he knocked at the door before going to open it.

In the farmyard it was unusually quiet. There were no dogs, no farm machinery. The farmhouse was so rundown that Jack thought it must be empty, then he saw that there was washing on the line. There were long discoloured bloomers, tent-like nightdresses and grey sheets. Jack found the silence and the space unnerving. He was aware of the vast sweep of the countryside behind him. It gave him a sense of vertigo. He wished Miss Hunt would let him in. He would feel more at ease in the small rooms of the bungalow.

'Mr Robson,' she said haughtily, feigning surprise. 'Whatever are you doing here?'

'I need to talk to you,' he said. He moved inside the porch and felt happier, sheltered from the space outside. 'It's a private matter,' he said more confidently. 'I didn't want to discuss it at school.'

She still would not let him into the house. 'If you have any problems about work,' she said, 'it would be much better, don't you think, to discuss them on Monday morning?'

'I don't have any problem,' he said. He was confused by her

attitude. Previously he had always found her so helpful and understanding. Perhaps the power of running the school has gone to her head, he thought.

'It's about Mr Medburn,' he said. 'I think you know more about him than you've told the police.'

Without a word she stood aside and let him in.

She took him into the kitchen and he chose a chair with his back to the sea. He felt safer that way. She must have been shopping because there was a cardboard box waiting to be unpacked on the table. She thought he might at least have waited to be invited to sit down and she remained standing, looking down at him, to make the point. He felt her hostility and realized that her privacy was important to her. Perhaps after all it would have been better to talk to her at school.

'Have you seen the newspapers?' he asked.

She nodded. 'Poor Kitty Medburn,' she said. 'They're making her out to be some kind of monster.'

He felt in his pocket for the comforting packet of cigarettes, but realized it would not do to light one.

'I don't think she killed Medburn,' he said. 'She wasn't that sort of coward.'

Irene Hunt raised her eyebrows. 'I think we would all have been capable of killing Harold Medburn,' she said.

'Was he blackmailing you?'

There, he thought, and I meant to be tactful.

She did not answer directly. 'I'm sorry,' she said coldly. 'I don't understand what business this is of yours.'

'Kitty Medburn's a friend,' he said. 'I'm going to prove that she's innocent.'

He thought for a moment that she was going to laugh. After all, who could blame her? He was a school caretaker, a retired miner with no education or skill. But she did not laugh. She turned away from him and filled a kettle with water.

'Wouldn't it be better to leave it to the police?' she asked.

'The police think Kitty killed him.'

Her back was still turned to him. She spooned tea into a pot.

'Was he blackmailing you?' Jack asked more gently.

'Yes,' she said. She sat slowly in a chair by the table. Her face was blank with thought.

'There was a woman who came to the church looking for you,' he said. 'Did that have something to do with it?'

She looked up suddenly, surprised, impressed perhaps that he had found out so much. She nodded.

'That was my daughter,' she said. 'My illegitimate daughter. She was born while I was still very young. I was seventeen. My parents persuaded me to place her for adoption. Then an act was passed which allowed adopted children to trace their natural mothers. Anne came to Heppleburn to look for me. She went to the church. I suppose she thought she could go there with confidence. And she met Harold Medburn.'

'Would it have been so dreadful,' Jack asked, 'if people knew that you had an illegitimate child?'

'No,' she said. 'Of course not. Not at that time. It would have been awkward and unpleasant but not so dreadful. I could have dealt with that. But he wasn't threatening me. He was threatening that he would tell Anne's family. Her husband hadn't wanted her to look for me. I'm not sure why. Perhaps he thought I must be a wicked woman who would bring depravity and destruction into his happy home. She had come to Heppleburn against his wishes and without his knowledge. The marriage wasn't a happy one but she was determined to sustain it because of the children. She confided all this to Harold Medburn on her first visit to the church. He told me that he would inform her husband that she had found me unless I paid him.' She looked seriously at Jack. 'I had betrayed my daughter once,' she said. 'I couldn't do it again.'

'And you've been paying him ever since?'

She nodded, and gave a sad, unnatural laugh. 'Do you know what's so ironic?' she said. 'There would have been no need to pay him any more. She had decided to separate from her husband. Her children have grown up so she doesn't feel the need to pretend any longer. I'd decided that I'd made my last payment and then

73

he died. I missed the satisfaction of telling him he wouldn't get more money from me.'

He knew she would want no sympathy.

'Can I speak to your daughter?' he asked.

'No,' she said. 'I'll not have her involved in this. You'll have to trust that what I've told you is true.'

Jack tried to remember when Miss Hunt had first come to the school. The village had been more isolated then and he thought it must have been a big event, the arrival of an attractive young woman. He could not picture her, but could remember the gossip that surrounded her, the excitement she had generated. She had spoken differently from them. In post-war austerity her clothes had been expensive, the envy of all the local women.

'You aren't local,' he said. 'You didn't come from the north-east.'

'No,' she said bitterly. 'My parents banished me from the civilized world.'

'Who was the father of your child?'

He realized at once that he had made a mistake. She was white with anger. 'That's an impertinence!' she cried. He was a child again, reprimanded for a rudeness he had never intended. 'The father of my child has no relevance to this. He would never be mixed up with anything so sordid.'

'I'm sorry,' he said. 'I didn't mean to upset you.' He longed to take a cigarette from the packet in his coat pocket, but was afraid of provoking her to more anger. He saw then that she had begun to cry.

'I loved him,' she said. 'There hasn't been a day for forty years when I've not thought about him.'

How sad, he thought, how pathetic to be so obsessed with the past.

'Then you'll understand,' he said, 'why I need to help Kitty.'

'Yes,' she said softly. 'I suppose I understand.'

She stood up briskly and dried her eyes on a large white handkerchief. She brought a teapot and two mugs to the table. The admission that they had something important in common encouraged him. He took it for granted now that she would help him. She unpacked the brown cardboard box of shopping until she found a fruit cake. She cut two slices and handed one to him on a brown earthenware plate.

'When I first came to Heppleburn I tried to make friends with Kitty Medburn,' she said. 'Harold was assistant master at the school then and we were a similar age. But she seemed suspicious of me. She made it clear that I wasn't welcome in their home. I found it hurtful. Everything here was so strange and I felt completely alone.'

'That would have been Harold,' he said. 'Kitty wouldn't have meant to be unkind.'

'Perhaps.'

He wanted to make the most of her new cooperation and refused to be distracted by her memories.

'Did you go into Medburn's room on Saturday afternoon?' he asked.

She thought. 'Yes,' she said. 'I needed more Sello-tape to put up the decorations. He always kept a hoard in his desk.'

'Did you see the gown there?'

'I don't know,' she said. 'The police have asked me that and I can't remember.'

'Did you notice if anyone else went into the office?'

She shook her head. 'How was he killed?' she asked suddenly. 'I don't understand what happened.'

He shrugged. 'I don't know,' he said helplessly.

'Why don't you ask Ramsay?'

'I don't like to.'

'That's ridiculous!' she said, turning into a teacher again. 'You won't get Kitty free with that attitude.'

'I don't think I'm very good at this,' he said. 'Perhaps I should leave it to the police after all.'

'Don't give up,' she said. She felt sorry for him. She had never realized before how sensitive he was. He had been a little man in a brown overall who mended the school's central heating. But she could not believe that his investigation would produce a result.

'Come on,' she said. 'I'll drive you to the bus stop.'

She led him out to the farmyard. A small boy with a dog was

driving cows in to be milked. The sun was a big orange ball low over the Cheviots. She drove him to the main road and left him, stranded in the countryside, in the magic orange light.

Angela Brayshaw had planned her day meticulously. It was the only way she could live. She was frightened by chaos and the unexpected. She would take the bus to Whitley Bay to shop in the morning, bake in the afternoon and later she would take her daughter to the firework display on the recreation ground. She was still in her dressing gown when Paul Wilcox telephoned. The whispered phone call, his desperate entreaty to meet her, disturbed and irritated her. It was upsetting because it was so unexpected. It had been a long time since she had been alone with Paul Wilcox. She had thought the affair was all over. In these matters she was always the passive partner. It never occurred to her to wonder if she loved. To be loved was important. To be the object of adoration was to be in a position of power. Paul Wilcox had never adored her but had seemed to need her, he had been physically attracted to her. Then his conscience had got the better of him. More recently, whenever he saw her he looked timid and ashamed.

'I'm not sure I can see you today,' she said. 'I'm very busy.' She was irritated because she might have to rearrange her plans. Besides, she knew he would insist on meeting her.

'Please,' he said. 'Hannah will be out this afternoon. I was going to take the children to the park. I could meet you there, as if by chance . . .'

'I don't know,' she said. But she was flattered by his attention and desperation. It occurred to her suddenly that he might be of some use. He could lend her money, so she could pay at least some of what she owed to her mother. She was convinced that she only had to buy time, that there would be no need now to join her mother in the old people's home. She was already deciding which clothes to wear, what make-up to use.

In the afternoon he was at the park before her. There were more people than she had expected: dog walkers, bored teenagers, rowdy children. If Wilcox had been hoping for privacy he would be disappointed. A group of boys was hovering around the bonfire. They were as fascinated as if it were already alight and prodded it, and threw bits of wood onto the top of it. Paul Wilcox was pushing his little girl on the swing. The boy was on the climbing frame absorbed in some game of his own. As she approached she thought derisively how pathetic Wilcox was. What sort of a man was he? He allowed his wife to dominate him, to go out to work, to take all the decisions in the house. Even when he was employed he had been a nurse, which was women's work. Harold Medburn had been more of a man than him. But perhaps now Paul had come to his senses, she thought. He had decided how much he needed her. Well, she would make him pay for his pleasure.

Paul Wilcox had been looking out for her, but pretended not to notice her until she came quite close to him.

'Hello,' he said. His voice was so falsely cheerful that even the child in the swing turned round to see what was wrong.

'What a surprise,' she said, leaning against one of the metal supports of the swing, 'to see you here!'

Her voice was softly seductive but she found it impossible to keep the sneer from it. His reaction surprised her. She had considered him humiliated, crawling back to her to ask for her favours, but he was angry, accusing.

'You told Harold Medburn about us,' he said. 'It was a despicable thing to do.'

'Why?' she said. 'Are you ashamed? You seemed to enjoy making love to me.'

'Be quiet,' he said, looking anxiously at his daughter, his anger collapsing with embarrassment.

'I was lonely,' he said. 'Frustrated. You took advantage of that.'

It was her turn to pretend to righteous anger.

'I don't remember it that way at all,' she said. 'You asked me into your house for a cup of coffee after a Parents' Association meeting. I accepted. You didn't tell me that your wife was working away. It wasn't my fault that I never drank the coffee.'

'I'm sorry,' he muttered. 'You're right. I'm to blame for the mess.'

She looked at him in disgust. It was astonishing now to believe that she'd had such hopes of the relationship. He had been kind, touchingly eager to please. And he had lived in such a beautiful house. She would have done almost anything to live in a house like that. But he had never really been her type. Almost immediately after they had begun to meet regularly he had started to discuss his wife. It had irritated Angela intensely. He still loved Hannah, he said, more than anyone else in the world. What a bastard he was to carry on like this! She had hoped he would lose the romantic obsession with his wife, but it had come as no surprise when he stopped inviting her back for coffee after the meetings, stopped dropping into her home during the day when Lizzie was at the toddler group. There had been no explanation. Fortunately there had been no emotional scenes. She had taken the rejection philosophically and turned her whole attention to Harold Medburn.

'You didn't tell me it was supposed to be a secret,' she said, trying to provoke him to anger again.

'I thought it was obvious!'

There was a silence. 'Let's not argue,' she said then. She stood close beside him and touched his arm. The attempt to excite him was habitual, given purpose now by her need for money. 'We used to be such good friends. Tell me what Harold did to upset you.'

'He tried to blackmail me,' Wilcox said. He was too humiliated at first to say that Medburn had succeeded. The little girl screamed to be let out of the swing. He lifted her out and watched her run off to play with the other children. Wilcox continued speaking, becoming more heated and confused as he talked: 'It seemed incredible. He was a headmaster. I couldn't believe it. He told me that he was going to tell Hannah about you and me. He thought it was his moral duty. When I said there was nothing to tell, he said he had proof. It might be possible to come to some arrangement, he said. I could support one of his charities. It was ridiculous but I believed in his charity at first. He was a church warden, after all. Then he wanted more money and when I refused he threatened to talk to Hannah. He was going to see her at the Hallowe'en party, he said. He'd have a little chat with her then.'

For a moment she said nothing and the lack of reaction made the rush of words seem ludicrous.

Angela Brayshaw smiled unpleasantly. 'Perhaps you had better tell the police,' she said. 'If he were blackmailing you, you had a reason to kill him.'

'No!' he was shocked.

'I bet you were relieved when he didn't turn up at the party.'

'Of course,' he said, 'but that doesn't mean ...' He lapsed unhappily into silence again, then said suddenly: 'Could he have had proof? You wouldn't have given him my letters, the poetry I wrote for you?'

'Wouldn't I?' she said, enjoying his discomfort. 'You'll never know now, will you?' She walked close to him again so their shoulders were almost touching. 'I need help,' she said. 'I need money myself.'

'You bitch!' he shouted, losing all control, almost hysterical in his temper. 'You think you can try the same trick as Medburn. Well you'll never blackmail me. No one will believe you. They all know you're a whore. You're an evil little bitch!'

She only laughed at him, a cruel, humourless laugh, her head thrown back, her pointed chin high in the air.

They were so engrossed in the argument that neither of them had seen Jack Robson approaching on his way home from the bus stop. He looked different, suddenly elderly, his hands deep in his macintosh pockets, his head bent in thought. Even when he drew close to them they did not quite recognize him. But Wilcox's shout made Robson look up quickly, so that they knew who it was, and the three of them stood in embarrassed silence, until Robson nodded his head in greeting and walked on. By then it was almost dark and quite cold. Wilcox shivered, called to the children and hurried away without speaking or looking at Angela again. She watched him until he disappeared into the dusk. His back was stooped over his daughter's pushchair, so that from her perspective he seemed deformed. She pulled her coat tightly around her and walked past the menacing silhouette of the bonfire on her way home.

In Jack Robson's house, on the door mat, there was a letter from Kitty. It was in a thin, pale blue envelope and written on prison notepaper with a number stamped on the top. His hand was shaking as he opened it. It might have been a first love letter. Then, with a kind of superstition, he decided it would be wrong to read it immediately. He left it on his dining room table, lit the fire and put on his slippers. He drew all the curtains and made himself tea. Then he sat by the fire and gave the letter his full attention.

It was an old-fashioned flowing script. It had a formality which distressed him. Why did she write as if he were a mere acquaintance? He could have been an employee. Did she feel she could not trust him? At the end he was not sure exactly what she meant to say. The letter was an anticlimax.

Dear Mr Robson,
I would like to thank you for your kindness to me on the night of my husband's murder. You must forgive my foolishness. You must not concern yourself about my welfare. Everyone here has been most considerate and I do not need anything.

Yours,
Kathryn Medburn

As Jack read the letter for a second time he realized that it was a form of dismissal. He was angry and refused to accept it. He decided he would take Miss Hunt's advice and he went to look for Ramsay.

Northumberland police's B Division spread from the old pit villages of the south-east plain to the rural wildness of the inland hills. Its headquarters were in Otterbridge, in the middle of the region. Otterbridge was a stately county town with a ruined abbey, a wide, slow-flowing river and walls which had once protected it from Scottish brigands. The police station was in the middle of the town. It was an ugly red-brick building, extended into a modern block where the communications centre was housed. Ramsay's office was at the top of the old building with a view of the sheep market and the moors. The surface of the desk was clear. Once he had kept a photograph of his wife there, but since Diana had left he preferred things uncluttered. He could hear Hunter's voice above all the others in the large communal office at the other side of the glass door. The sergeant had just come in but already had the others listening to his stories, laughing at his jokes. Ramsay opened the glass door and the outer office fell silent.

'Gordon,' he said quietly, 'could you spare a moment?'

Hunter sauntered in and leaned against the window sill, as if Ramsay was hardly worth his attention. Ramsay shut the door carefully behind him.

'I think we can soon close the Medburn case,' he said. 'The pathologist's report seems to tie it up.'

That's good, Hunter thought. He might make that date with the nurse from the Freeman after all. But he pretended interest. He was ambitious in his own way. He wanted an inspector's salary.

'How's that then?' he asked.

'Medburn was drugged before he was strangled with his own tie,' Ramsay said. 'The business with the noose was a charade. The pathologist found traces of Heminevrin in the body. It's a medicine used in the control of alcohol addiction. It's also taken by old people to help them sleep. As a district nurse Mrs Medburn worked a lot with elderly people in their own homes.'

'Did she give them the Heminevrin herself?' Hunter asked.

'Not officially. She wouldn't have had access to it directly. It's a controlled drug only available on doctor's prescription, but she often went to the chemist's to collect her patients' medicines. Apparently it would only have taken three teaspoons to knock out Medburn. He took it on an empty stomach and that would have made it work more quickly. Mrs Medburn could easily have taken that much from a bottle of syrup without her patient noticing. All we need is the information that one of her regular patients has been prescribed the drug recently.' He looked at Hunter. 'You can do that,' he said. 'It'll not take long.'

'Won't it wait until tomorrow?'

'Let's get it wrapped up tonight,' Ramsay said. 'I thought you needed the overtime.'

'Slave-driver,' Hunter said, only half joking. As he left the office the phone was ringing.

At first Ramsay did not recognize Jack Robson's name. He had thought of the old man only as Patty Atkins's father.

'I need to talk to you,' Robson said. 'When can I see you?' Ramsay looked at his watch.

'I could come to Heppleburn now,' he said, 'if it's urgent.'

'Aye,' Robson said. 'It's urgent all right.'

'Will I come to your home?'

'Where else? I don't live with my daughter, you know, I'm a grown man.'

When Ramsay arrived at the house in the quiet, ordered street Jack was waiting for him, the fire made up, the room tidy. Ramsay was determined not to antagonize Robson. He sat where he was told.

'Now,' he said. 'How can you help me?'

'I don't know that I can,' Jack said. Now that Ramsay was in his house he felt awkward and the embarrassment came out as hostility. 'Not yet. I need information. How did Medburn die?'

Ramsay considered. Jack thought he would refuse to tell him and prepared to be angry.

'I'll tell you,' Ramsay said at last. 'There'll be a press statement tomorrow anyway. He was drugged with a medicine called Heminevrin which is used to treat old people.' He paused, then continued a little apologetically: 'It's just the evidence we needed to convict Mrs Medburn. She would have had access to the drug through her patients. We'll probably be closing the case tomorrow.'

'Why tomorrow?' Robson demanded. 'If you're so certain, why haven't you closed it already?'

'We need to confirm that one of Mrs Medburn's patients was taking the drug.'

'If you've not done that yet, there's no proof,' Robson exclaimed. 'You're being a bit hasty, man. What about all the other folk who could get hold of it? This estate is full of old people. The bathrooms are full of pills and potions and no one would notice if a bottle was missing. And what about Angela Brayshaw? She's always in and out of her mother's nursing home. I expect they use that medicine there.'

He stopped abruptly, realizing how desperate he sounded.

'We'll check, of course,' Ramsay said, 'but I think you should prepare yourself to accept the fact that Kitty Medburn killed her husband.'

Robson did not answer. Ramsay felt he had been misled. The old man had brought him all the way to Heppleburn under false pretences. He had no useful information at all. He was an infatuated old fool who could not believe that a childhood sweetheart was capable of murder. Well, he would have no part in his games. When he spoke again it was with brisk formality.

'Heminevrin has a very unpleasant taste,' he said. 'You can't think how Medburn was persuaded to drink the stuff? Even in coffee it must have been very bitter.'

'Medburn didn't have much of a sense of taste,' Jack said, despite himself. 'He had a lot of sinus trouble.' Then he added quickly: 'Everyone who came to the school knew that. He was always complaining about it. It doesn't mean Kitty killed him.'

'Why did you ask to talk to me?' Ramsay said, his patience suddenly at an end. 'Have you any new information or is this all a waste of time? If you know anything it's your duty to pass it on.'

'My duty is to the people I represent,' Robson cried. 'I've nothing to tell you. Not yet. Unless I find proof you'll never let Kitty go. You're only interested in getting a result.'

'No,' Ramsay said quietly. 'That's not true. I'm not that sort of policeman.'

Robson wanted to believe him. There was a great temptation to share the responsibility, to tell Ramsay that Wilcox was frightened of Medburn, that Miss Hunt was a blackmail victim, that he had seen Wilcox and Angela Brayshaw together in the park. It was only stubbornness and an habitual distrust of the police which kept him silent. He was confused and did not know how best Kitty could be helped.

Ramsay was irritated by Robson's determined silence, but he would not allow himself to be roused to anger. Why had he given up valuable time to talk to the old man? He had gained nothing but the information that Harold Medburn had suffered from a blocked nose. Robson's obsession with Kitty Medburn's innocence was foolish. It was time for the police to get out of Heppleburn and leave the matter to the courts. But as he left the council house and drove back to Otterbridge he felt a sudden unease. Robson's certainty had undermined his own judgement. He hoped Hunter had found the evidence to link Kitty Medburn to the drug which had made her husband unconscious. And he wished he had persuaded Robson to talk to him.

Chapter Seven

All the village was at the bonfire. Mothers carried babies as fat as Eskimos with extra clothes and even the old men from the Miners' Welfare cottages stood in the comfort of the cricket pavilion to watch the fireworks. When Ramsey drove back through the village towards Otterbridge, the streets were deserted and the Northumberland Arms was empty.

Matthew Carpenter had been asked to supervise the event and he left his flat early. In the chemist shop below the lights were still on, though the door was locked. The pharmacist was checking medicines against a list on a clipboard and looked up to wave at him. Although Matthew arrived at the bonfire half an hour before it was scheduled to start groups of older boys were there before him, prodding the bonfire and annoying each other. When they saw Matthew approaching they fell silent. They treated him with respect, not because he was a teacher at the little school, but because he had been in the school on the night of the murder. They were fascinated by the macabre and melodramatic manner of Harold Medburn's death. The murder was a vast video nasty, performed in the village for their entertainment. They talked about it in giggled whispers, creating grotesque fantasies, then accused each other of being scared.

As soon as he arrived on the field Matthew sensed that some mischief was being planned. He was an inexperienced teacher but the furtive conversations and nervous bravado brought back memories of his own boyhood.

'I won't have any messing about with fireworks,' he said firmly.

'It's dangerous and there'll be too many people here tonight. We don't want accidents.'

He was surprised by the authority in his voice and the boys' easy agreement. He spoke to a group of three, uniform shapes in his torchlight. He did not know their names.

'We've not got fireworks of our own,' one said. 'It's not allowed. There's a display.'

'That's all right then.'

It was seven o'clock. A huge moon was rising above the silhouettes of the trees. It lit the bonfire and the faces of the boys.

'Aren't you having a guy?' Matthew asked. 'When I was a kid we always had a guy.'

The boys sniggered and did not reply. Matthew reminded himself that they were only young – perhaps no older than eleven or twelve – unsure of themselves as newcomers in the comprehensive school.

'Well?' he demanded.

'Aye sir. We made one earlier.' The one who spoke was braver than the rest and the others collapsed again in giggles.

'Well,' Matthew said again. 'Where is it?'

They looked at each other. This obviously had not been part of the plan. The silence of their hesitation was broken by the sound of people walking down the footpath from the village, of laughter and children's voices.

'Come on!' Matthew said, becoming increasingly impatient. 'People are coming. We want the guy on the top of the bonfire before everyone gets here.' But he realized that he was already too late for that. Family parties were starting to congregate on the edge of the field. The organizers were beginning to set out their stalls for hot dogs and drinks. In a roped-off corner of the field rockets were being set into bottles.

The boys, looking sheepish, realized that the game was over. They disappeared and returned some minutes later pushing a pram with a guy propped inside. The head and body were made in the conventional way – a pillowcase was stuffed with newspaper and old stockings and tied with string to make the neck – but it was dressed in a black pointed hat made of cardboard and wrapped around with a long black cloak. One of the boys' mothers had obviously been to the school's Hallowe'en party.

'What's the meaning of the costume?' Matthew demanded. He felt embarrassed. A crowd was already gathering around them. He knew the point the boys were trying to make, but to recognize it would give the idea some credibility. It would be to admit that he too thought Kitty Medburn was a witch.

'It's a witch,' the smallest boy said;

'I can see that.'

'They used to burn witches,' another said.

'Not on bonfire night.'

'After what was in the paper,' the same boy said. He was more cocky and articulate than the others. 'We thought it would be . . .' he hesitated to find the right word '. . . topical.'

'Well I call it stupid. Take the costume off and let's get the guy to the top of the bonfire. Which of you is going to climb up?'

Matthew could tell that the crowd around him had heard the exchange with the boys and he felt threatened by its response. He felt a suppressed tension and hostility in the watching people. Was it because he had allowed the prank to develop in the first place? Or because he had prevented its conclusion and so deprived the onlookers of the ritual spectacle of the witch's burning. He could not tell. He put the cloak and hat into the pram and moved it away from the fire, then lifted the smallest boy up so that he could wedge the guy at the top of the woodpile.

Jack Robson had been expected for tea at Patty's house, and when he had failed to arrive she became concerned and drove over to see him. She found him still in the chair by the fire where he had sat to reconsider Kitty's letter after seeing Ramsay into the street. He seemed not to have heard her come in. He was feeling as lost and unsure of himself as he had in the empty dramatic countryside near Miss Hunt's bungalow.

'Dad,' she said. She bounded into the room and squatted on the floor beside him, looking more like a friendly, badly-trained dog than ever. 'Aren't you coming to the bonfire?'

'No,' he said. 'I don't think I'll come.'

'But you must. The bairns are expecting you.'

'All right,' he said, too tired even to stand up to her. The argument with Ramsay had taken all the fight from him. 'I'll be ready in five minutes.'

'There's no hurry,' she said. 'Tell me what happened at Miss Hunt's.'

He looked up from Kitty's letter. A lot seemed to have happened since his encounter with Irene Hunt.

'She was being blackmailed by Medburn,' he said flatly. 'It was as we thought. The woman in the church was an illegitimate daughter. Medburn had threatened to tell the woman's husband, who hadn't wanted her to look for her mother.'

'There you are then!' Patty was enthusiastic and seemed not to recognize how hurt her father was. 'Miss Hunt had motive, opportunity. All we have to do is tell Ramsay.'

'No,' he said bending to lace up his shining black boots, looking up at her as he pulled hard on the laces to tighten them before fastening the knot. 'Miss Hunt's daughter has recently separated from her husband. Miss Hunt herself is about to retire. She had nothing more to fear from Medburn. She had no reason to kill him.'

'I see.' Her enthusiasm was momentarily dampened but her usual optimism soon returned. 'All the same,' she said, 'at least it shows that Kitty Medburn wasn't the only person who wanted Medburn dead. Don't you think we should tell Ramsay?'

'I don't know,' he said. 'I spoke to him this evening. I found out how Medburn died. He was drugged, then strangled. He was already dead before he was strung up on the hoop.'

'But you didn't tell him you've been talking to Paul Wilcox and Miss Hunt?'

'No,' He could think of nothing now but the cold rejection of Kitty's letter. 'We won't do anything yet. It said in the paper it could be months before she comes to trial. There's no hurry.'

She did not have his patience and wanted the thing decided, but knew it would do no good to argue. She took his arm and helped him to the car, then they walked with Jim and the children to the bonfire. Because Jack had delayed them they were late arriving and the bonfire was already lit; sparks flew high towards the moon and flames were licking around the bare-bodied guy.

When Angela Brayshaw collected her daughter from her mother she felt nothing. The meeting with Paul Wilcox had drained her. She was emotionally and physically exhausted. And then her mother had begun to talk again about money.

'I must press you, dear,' Mrs Mount said, 'for a starting date. We're terribly short-handed. Shall we say next Monday?'

'All right!' Angela said crossly. 'All right!'

The sense of expectation and optimism which had been with her since Medburn's death had left her. If she were to benefit from his death she would surely have heard something by now. She had lost all hope. There was nothing left but the nursing home and a return to the dependence on her mother. She had forgotten all about the bonfire, and Claire's excitement about the evening irritated her. She even tried to persuade the girl that they should stay at home but knew from the beginning that it would be no good. Claire could be as stubborn as her mother, and Angela was in no mood for dealing with tantrums. They walked down the footpath towards the field. Claire pulled her mother by the arm to hurry her and they were among the first to arrive. They stood on the frosty grass with the rest of the crowd and watched the boys' confrontation with Matthew Carpenter.

'Why is the guy dressed like a witch?' Claire asked.

'I don't know.'

'Why is Mr Carpenter making them take off the costume?'

'Stop asking so many foolish questions.'

Angela turned away. They would like to burn me as a witch, she thought, all these respectable, complacent, contented families. She had not read the papers. She did not know what the thing was all about. As she walked away from the fire she saw Irene Hunt watching her and the boys with disapproval. Stuck-up old cow! she thought, remembering the hints Harold Medburn had given her about Irene's past. She pretends to be so superior and she's no better than I am. What's she doing here anyway? Keeping an eye on that young teacher to stop him getting drunk again, I suppose. Angela walked further on and saw the Wilcox family on their way down from the mill. Hannah was pushing the baby in a smart buggy and Paul was carrying the little boy on his shoulders. It was a picture of domestic idyll. She watched them with hatred and envy and wished they were all dead.

All evening Jack Robson watched the firework display without enthusiasm. What had Kitty been trying to tell him? That after all she had killed her husband? Or that even if she were released she would never return his affection? The display was halfway through. Andrew and Jennifer had badgered their mother to buy them baked potatoes and he was standing alone. He looked up the hill to the three silhouettes— the church, the school and the school house – which stood against the clear sky. Even from this distance it seemed that the light from the bonfire was being reflected in the windows of the buildings on the hill. Jack looked again, and realized that the light in the school house was not reflected flame. It came from inside and was the sharp spot of torchlight. He was tempted to do nothing, to turn his back on it and go to find his grandchildren. He would spend the evening watching their pleasure in the fireworks. He would forget about Kitty Medburn. He was a retired miner and a school caretaker and nothing else was his business.

But even as he was thinking that, he was pulling his scarf from his coat pocket and winding it around his neck, because it would be cold away from the fire, and he was wondering how long he could be away before Patty noticed he had gone. He walked quickly up the dark alley towards the school. Halfway up the hill he stopped and turned round, convinced for a moment that he was being followed. The path twisted and was in shadow and he could not see very far, but he told himself that it was his imagination. There was no sound of footsteps, no noise at all, except the machine-gun rattle of a rocket as it splintered into coloured stars in the sky.

There were no cars in the playground. The school house door was firmly locked. There was no light now inside the house, but it has been impossible to walk quietly over the yard and whoever was inside would have been warned that he was there. Again Jack felt the sensation of being followed but when he looked round there was nothing except the moonlight shining through the wire mesh fence which surrounded the playing field, making a lacy pattern of shadow on the grass. There were lights in the vicarage windows and from an upstairs window the sound of a crying baby. The sound was comforting.

Jack walked slowly round the house to the back where there was a small gloomy garden, a sagging, washing line and an outside toilet. The kitchen window was wide open. Surely the police would never have left it like that, gaping, an invitation to burglars. At one time he would have climbed in through there – the window was big enough and the sill was only three feet from the ground – but he was too old and sensible for that kind of escapade now. He felt in his coat pocket for a bunch of school keys. He was sure he had a spare house key as part of the set. He walked slowly back to the front door.

He put the key in the lock and it turned stiffly. Inside the hall he hesitated. There seemed, no reason why he should not put on the electric light. The intruder, if there was an intruder, would know by now that he was there. All the same he was reluctant to touch the switch as if he was frightened by what the sudden light would reveal. In the event when he touched the switch nothing happened. He presumed that the electricity board had been informed that the house was empty and had switched the power off at the mains. He had no torch and had to depend on the faint gleam from outside and the sudden coloured glare of fireworks. He went first into the small back room where he had taken Kitty on the night of the murder. It already smelled musty, as if the damp which had been held at bay with coal fires and open windows had taken over. Beyond was the kitchen, which was old-fashioned, even primitive, like the kitchen Joan had had when they were first married. There was lino on the floor and a square table with an oil cloth cover. A wooden airer which could be let down from the ceiling with a rope and pulley still held a thin tea towel. What a mean bastard

Medburn had been! Jack thought. He had spent nothing on the house. Instead he must have saved all his money for his fancy woman.

Anger began to dispel his fear and he walked into the front room, where an upright piano stood against one wall, the lid up, the keys gleaming and chilly like teeth. On top of the piano was a wedding photograph. Jack took it to the window and held it towards the light so he could see the detail. Medburn looked as smug as if he had won the pools. Kitty was poised and still and stared fixedly at the camera. He replaced the photograph. In a corner of the room was a dressmaker's dummy, wearing the body of a blouse, stuck with pins. This must have been Kitty's room, he thought. She came here to sew in peace. He felt her presence as strongly as if she were in the room with him.

There was a noise from upstairs, a faint nervous noise of a throat being cleared.

'Who's there?' Jack shouted. 'Who are you? Is it the police?'

There was no reply and Jack went up the stairs. He was halfway up when the front door, which he had left wide open, to let light into the house, banged shut. As he climbed the stairs Jack remembered suddenly his first day down the pit. His dad had told him what it would be like – the men squashed into the cage, the heat, the dark, the speed of descent, but he had been too dull then, too cocky, to have any imagination and the thing itself had come as a complete shock. He had come through it without showing fear and the memory that he had not let himself down in front of the other lads kept him going as he came to the top of the stairs and walked onto the landing. He was as proud and foolhardy as he had been as a boy.

He stood on the landing and pushed open the first door he came to with his boot. The moon was shining right into the room and it was light enough to see every detail, to see even to read. There were no curtains at the window. It had never been used as a bedroom. It had been, Jack thought, some kind of study. There was a big, old-fashioned desk under the window with papers scattered all over it. Jack approached the desk to see more clearly.

First he picked up a small scrap of paper with Irene Hunt's name and address written on it. It caught his attention because the address was not local and he put it into his pocket to look at later. The paper was so small that it would not be missed. He was about to sort through the larger items, which he could tell now were letters, when he heard a noise behind him and he was hit on the head. He fell unconscious to the floor.

He woke to bright torchlight and the sound of his name being called.

'Dear me, Mr Robson,' Ramsay said. 'You'll really have to take more care of yourself.'

Jack tried to sit up and was sick. Even then, through the giddiness, he saw that the desk was empty and that all the letters had disappeared.

'What are you doing here?' he demanded. The loss of dignity annoyed him. He felt that the policeman was in some way to blame for his humiliation.

'I've had a man keeping an eye on the place as part of his patrol. He saw that the front door was open.' Ramsay helped Jack to his feet and into the bathroom. 'I should ask you what you're doing here,' he said. 'But that can wait for a while.'

Alone in the bathroom Jack was sick again, then washed his face and hands and felt better. Ramsay was waiting tactfully on the landing.

'Someone hit me,' Jack said. He was too angry to keep anything from the police now. Besides it would be impossible otherwise to explain what he was doing here. 'Somebody bloody hit me.'

Ramsay took his arm and began to walk him slowly down the stairs.

'Come and sit down,' he said. 'You can tell me about it then.'

He led Jack into the front room and sat him in a big armchair. Jack looked around him. The room seemed for some reason different. It was as if a great time had elapsed since he had been there. Only then did he realize that Ramsay must have switched on the electricity at the mains because the room was lit by a tall standard lamp with a pink shade, and the curtains were drawn.

'I was looking at the letters on the desk upstairs,' he said, 'and some bugger came up behind me and hit me on the head.'

'Letters?' Ramsay asked. 'Are you sure? There are no letters on the desk now. When we searched the house after Medburn's death there were a lot of papers in the drawers but nothing that was relevant to the inquiry. And there was nothing on top of the desk.'

'Someone was in the house before me,' Robson said impatiently. 'I don't suppose your policeman noticed that. They'd got in through the kitchen window. I opened the door with my spare key.'

'Why didn't you leave well alone and phone me?' It was the policeman's turn to sound angry. 'Whatever possessed you to wander around playing detective?'

'I'm the caretaker. It's my job.'

'Don't be a fool, man. You must have realized it could be dangerous.'

Ramsay looked at the little man huddled in the big chair on the other side of the room and wondered if he was mad.

'I love Kitty Medburn,' Robson said.

The declaration sounded desperate, moving and a little ridiculous. Ramsay had the same reaction as he would have done hearing six-year-olds swearing undying love in a school playground.

'And I don't think she killed her husband.'

'Why?' Ramsay asked.

'Because I know her. She would never do a thing like that.' He realized that the emotional outburst would never convince the policeman and tried to calm himself. 'Harold Medburn was a blackmailer,' he said. 'I know he was getting money out of Irene Hunt, and Paul Wilcox was frightened of him too. I heard Wilcox and Angela Brayshaw in the park this afternoon. Perhaps she had an affair with him before she moved on to Medburn.' He felt suddenly weak. 'I shouldn't have told you about Miss Hunt,' he said. 'The information was given me in confidence.'

'Away man!' For the first time the policeman raised his voice. 'You can't go snooping round in a village like this without people getting hurt. If you're right and Kitty Medburn isn't a killer then there's someone here who is. Do you want to protect them too?'

'I don't know,' Jack Robson said. He was no longer sure of anything.

'You'd better tell me everything you know.'

So Robson told the whole story, starting with his conversation with Kitty Medburn on the night of the party. He spoke slowly first, but then the words came easily. Ramsay was a good listener and it was a relief to tell it.

'So your daughter's involved in all this too?'

Jack nodded.

'I would have thought she'd have better things to do.'

'She wanted to come to you. I told her not to.'

'You'd have saved yourself a bump on the head.'

'Aye.' Jack grinned suddenly. 'Perhaps it's knocked some sense into me.'

'I doubt it.' It was hard not to like the man. Ramsay did not want to raise his expectations, then hurt him again. 'You know,' he said, 'it's still most likely that Kitty killed her husband. Despite what happened tonight.'

'Perhaps,' Robson said. He looked directly at the policeman. 'Did you read all those papers in the drawers upstairs?'

The policeman hesitated. 'No,' he said. 'We were sure, you see, that Mrs Medburn had killed her husband.' He paused again. 'It was a mistake.'

'Aye,' Jack Robson said bitterly. 'And now it's too late. The letters have gone.'

There was a silence. It was the only form of apology he would receive.

'It's like the Heminevrin,' Jack said suddenly. It had been on his mind, a growing grievance. 'You've not bothered to find out who else could get it. You assumed it was Kitty.'

'We're still making inquiries,' Ramsay said. 'Really.' He could not tell if Jack believed him, but it was true. Hunter had yet to find one of Kitty Medburn's patients who was taking the syrup. 'I'd like your help,' he said. 'I want you to go and see Kitty Medburn.'

'I don't know that she'll see me,' Jack said.

'Surely she would if you're such good friends . . . She must know you're trying to help her.'

'Why do you want me to see her?'

Ramsay chose his words carefully. 'She's a very self-contained woman,' he said. 'I find it hard to talk to her, to get through to her. Nothing seems to move her. If she did kill Harold Medburn it would be better for us all if she admitted it. It would certainly be better for her, and uncertainty places everyone under suspicion. That's uncomfortable. It makes people frightened, as you found out tonight. She might talk more freely to you.'

'You want me to make her confess,' Jack said, fierce and uncompromising, for an instant the gallant knight again protecting his lady. 'I'll not do it.'

'No!' Ramsay was almost shouting in his attempt to make the man understand. 'Talk to her. That's all. If you tell me then that she's innocent I'll take more notice. I trust you, you see, to be honest with me. You've a reputation to maintain.'

'I'm not sure she'll see me,' Jack muttered again, but he was thinking that he was not sure that he could face seeing her in that place. He thought she might blame him for the fact that she was there. He felt unreasonably that his show of affection on the night of the murder had in some way triggered the whole chain of events.

'But you will try?'

'Yes,' Jack said. 'I will try.' Not to help the policeman, but because he wanted to see her and be in the same room as her. He wanted to tell her how much he cared about her. He felt then that the interview was over, and prepared to lift himself to his feet.

'I'll have to go,' he said. 'Patty will be wondering where I am.'

'Just a few more minutes,' Ramsay said. 'I've already asked someone to tell your daughter' you're safe. There's something else. I need to ask some more questions.'

'I'm tired, man,' Jack said. His head was thumping. He wanted to sleep. 'Can't you tell I'm tired?'

'It's important. There's something I've not told you.'

'Away then.' He was too tired to argue. And it was restful there in the big chair. It seemed a terrible effort to move.

'When you first came into the house,' Ramsay asked, 'did you look downstairs?'

Jack nodded.

'In all the rooms?'

Jack nodded again. He seemed too exhausted to speak.

'Did you notice anything unusual?'

Jack shook his head. 'No,' he said. 'This room seems different but I can't think why.'

'I want to show you something,' Ramsay said. 'Can you walk with me into the kitchen?'

'I'm not an invalid, man,' Jack said with a flicker of the old spirit. 'I've a few years left yet.'

But as he stood up his head began to swim and he thought he might faint. He followed the policeman through the damp and gloomy back room to the kitchen. There, hanging by a noose made of washing line, attached to the wooden strut of the airer and swinging gently, was a figure in a black cloak and black painted hat. The figure turned towards them and Jack could see the smooth face and blank eyes. He began to shake.

'It's the dummy,' he said, desperately trying to keep control for it seemed to him that the policeman had intended to shock him into some indiscretion. 'It's the dressmaker's dummy. When I came into the house it was in the front room.'

Jack felt only relief. In his dazed state, when he had first come into the kitchen he had thought the figure was Kitty, that she had hung herself because he had let her down.

'There's a message for you,' Ramsay said, nodding in the direction of the window. There, on the glass, scrawled in lipstick in uneven capitals was written: 'Mind your own business.'

'The lipstick was Mrs Medburn's,' Ramsay said. 'It had been taken from the dressing table upstairs. Perhaps you had better do as you're told.'

He helped Jack to his car and as they drove away the picture of the figure remained with them. Neither could forget the smooth-skinned dummy dressed in the hat and cloak which had been removed from the bonfire guy earlier in the evening.

Chapter Eight

The remand centre car park was full. Sunday afternoon must have been a busy time for visiting. There was even a bus. In the queue at the gate into the prison there were babies clutching bottles and young women with picnic baskets. There was the feeling of a family day out. Inside the remand centre Jack Robson was separated from the other visitors. They were taken into a large noisy room, filled with smoke, where bored children roamed in packs. There was a tea bar at one end and the prison officers looked on with benign indifference.

'That won't do for you,' Ramsay said with a wink. 'You'll want a bit of privacy.'

Jack was whisked away. He followed a pretty young woman in a blue uniform down a series of identical corridors. Ramsay suddenly disappeared.

Kitty Medburn was wearing her own clothes – a thin wool jersey and a green plaid skirt. She was in a drab tiny interview room with her hands clasped on the table. Jack was not sure what he had expected. He had seen films where prisoners and visitors were separated by glass screens but there was none of that here. With sufficient courage he could have reached across the table immediately and taken her hands.

'Here you are, Mrs Medburn,' the officer said brightly as she opened the door. She might have been a nurse. 'I told you there was a visitor for you. I'll see if I can find you some tea.'

Then they were left alone.

Kitty had not moved as they came into the room. 'Jack,' she

said, looking at her hands. 'It was good of you to come to see me but there was no need.'

He felt that after all there was a glass screen between them. Her politeness and formality were a barrier which he was unable to break through.

'I had to come,' he said. 'I wanted to see you.'

'There was no need,' she said again, 'everyone here has been very thoughtful.'

'I didn't bring anything,' he said, wondering if he should have brought a present as if he were visiting someone sick in hospital. 'I didn't know what was allowed.'

She did not answer and there was an awkward, impenetrable silence.

'Kitty!' His voice was loud and cracked, and shattered the impression that there was nothing wrong. It was impossible to believe that she was an invalid in some exclusive clinic. 'Kitty, did you kill Harold?'

She looked at him directly for the first time with a peculiar cool disapproval.

'No,' she said. 'I didn't kill him.'

He was so relieved that he did not notice that she disapproved of his lack of control. 'I knew it,' he said, words bubbling from him like laughter. 'I told Ramsay that you'd never do anything like that.' He leaned forward over the table towards her. 'I've been carrying out my own investigation,' he said, 'talking to people. I'm already starting to get results. Patty's helping me.'

He saw suddenly that she was crying. There was no sound, no movement, but tears were rolling down her cheeks. They seemed to Jack as smooth and as pale as the face of the dressmaker's dummy.

'Dear Jack,' she said. 'You haven't changed at all.'

'Haven't I?' he said. He thought it was a compliment. 'I still care about you, Kitty. When you get out of here you'll see . . .'

'I don't know,' she said. There was panic in her voice but he was so desperate to make her realize that he was on her side that he did not recognize it.

'I'll have to ask you some questions,' Jack said. 'You won't mind, will you? It'll get you out of here more quickly. Ramsay's already started to reconsider the case, you know.' He sat back with pride. 'I've found new evidence, just by talking to people.'

She seemed confused. 'I didn't realize you were taking such an interest,' she said.

'You didn't think I'd do nothing!'

'I didn't realize,' she repeated.

'Did you know that Harold was a blackmailer?' He wished he had a notebook. She might take him more seriously if he had a notebook.

'No,' she said.

'You must have known that he was making money.'

'No,' she said. 'He always refused to discuss money with me. It was an obsession with him. He had several different bank accounts and he was always transferring money from one to another. He was secretive about it, but he always had been. We lived mostly on my wages.'

'Didn't you mind that?'

'No,' she said. 'There are different kinds of meanness.'

'Did it not occur to you that people were frightened of him?'

'No,' she said, 'I was never scared of him. I knew he wasn't well liked.'

'Harold was drugged with Heminevrin before he was strangled,' Jack said. 'Did the police tell you that?'

She nodded. 'They asked me where I got it.'

'Have you collected a prescription for Heminevrin for a patient recently?'

'No,' she said, 'but I had access to it. I helped out at Mrs Mount's nursing home the weekend before Harold died and they have it there to calm some of the old people.'

'Did you tell the police that?'

'No,' she said. 'I'd forgotten. But I'll tell them when they come again. I've nothing to hide.'

'Have you no idea who phoned him on the night of the murder?'

'No,' she said. 'I presumed it was his mistress. I didn't ask.'

She looked at him with affection and amusement. He felt so happy he could sing. 'I'm not a lot of help, am I?' she said.

'Why did you marry him?' he asked suddenly. It had nothing to do with the investigation. He was desperate to know.

'I thought it would work,' she said. 'I thought we would suit each other. It did work in a way. He gave me privacy. That was important. And security.'

'I would have married you,' he cried. 'You know I would have married you.'

'Yes,' she said. 'I knew that.'

'I've so many dreams,' he said. 'Just wait until you come home. We're so lucky to have found each other after all these years . . .'

She might have answered but the prison officer came in carrying two thick white cups three-quarters full of dark brown tea.

'I've put sugar in,' the young woman said. 'I thought you'd take sugar.'

She set the cups on the table and turned away, a dark plait swinging behind her, keys clanking at her side. The interruption threw Jack. The intimacy was suddenly lost. Perhaps he had presumed too much. The awkwardness between them had returned. Kitty seemed to withdraw into her own thoughts. She drank tea in silence. Her tears had dried on her cheeks. He coughed and she looked up sharply as if she had forgotten that he was still there.

'I think you should go,' she said. 'There are rules about visiting.'

'Of course,' he said. He stood up. He did not know if the door would be locked and what he should do to attract the prison officer's attention. 'Shall I come and see you again?' he asked.

'Not here,' she said.

'No,' he said. 'You're quite right. This isn't a good place to talk. We need time together. You'll be home soon.'

He wanted to lean over and kiss her smooth cheek, but the prison officer outside had seen that he was standing and had the door open. So he left the room without touching Kitty at all.

'Goodbye,' he said. 'I'll see you soon. You can depend on me.'

He was a proud, fierce little man, shorter than the woman who patiently held the door for him. Kitty remained sitting. She said nothing but she smiled at him.

Ramsay, waiting in the car, found Jack altered. He thought at first Kitty Medburn had confessed to the murder and it would all be over.

'What did she say?' he asked. He made no move to drive away.

'She didn't kill him,' Robson said, 'if that's what you're thinking. She's a truthful woman and she told me straight out.' He looked at Ramsay. 'She shouldn't be in a place like that,' he said. 'It's made her hard.'

'Did she tell you anything else?'

'Aye. She had access to that Heminevrin. They use it in Mrs Mount's old people's home, and she helped out there at weekends. I'm not betraying any confidence by telling you. She would have told you herself.'

Ramsay looked at the old man with sympathy. Don't get so involved, he wanted to say. That sort of infatuation is always destructive. I know. I loved Diana. The only way to survive is to stay detached. But he said only:

'Was she pleased to see you?'

Jack Robson flushed. 'Of course she was,' he said too loudly. 'We've always been friends.' As Ramsay started the engine, he added: 'Will you let her go?'

'No,' the inspector said. 'I can't do that. But I'll not close the case. Not yet.'

Patty Atkins felt angry and excluded for most of the day. When Kitty Medburn was arrested her father had asked for her help. They had become in a sense partners. Yet with a monumental folly and arrogance, without consulting her, he had wandered alone into the school house and been knocked unconscious. When Ramsay had helped him home the night before it had been as if Jack and the policeman were partners and she were fit for nothing better than making the tea. They told her nothing. She found out about the dummy dressed in the witch's costume, the possibility that there were two intruders, one who had been in the school house when

Jack had arrived and another who had followed him in, only by listening to their conversation. Mixed with anger there was guilt. She should have taken more care of her father. What would Ramsay think? That she was irresponsible and incompetent. It had come to matter a great deal what Ramsay thought.

On the Sunday morning her irritation persisted. Her father told her that Ramsay planned to arrange a visit for him to the remand centre but gave her no details. He wanted to go to the club with Jim for his usual Sunday morning drink, but she expressed her disapproval of the idea with a ferocity that surprised them both.

'I'm not spending all morning cooking a roast dinner only to have the pair of you too drunk to know what you're eating.'

They realized that she was upset, and surrendered without a fight. After all she never usually made a fuss about the club. They hung about the house, subdued and bored, until late morning when Jack said he had to go for a walk.

'Not far,' he said. 'I'll not go near the club. Just to the paper shop and back to stretch my legs.'

In fact he was gone for an hour, and she was beginning to become concerned. He arrived just as she was setting the meal on the table.

'Just as well you're back,' she said. 'It would have gone in the bin.'

Then the doorbell rang and Ramsay was standing there, tall and beautiful and apologetic.

'I've come to see your father,' he said. 'It's an awkward time. I'm sorry.'

'Have you eaten?' she asked. 'There's plenty.' Jack and her husband looked on with resentment. Why was she so pleasant to the policeman when she had been so unreasonably bad-tempered with them?

'Are you sure?' Ramsay asked. 'You're very kind.'

'Wait till you've tasted it before you say that,' Jack said spitefully. 'Our Patty's never been much of a cook.'

Ramsay sat at the table in a space squeezed between the children and ate everything put before him. He seemed not to mind that the beef was not as tender as it might have been or that the sprouts had begun to disintegrate. He liked his vegetables well-cooked, he said. And not to worry that the Yorkshire puddings were stuck to the pan. It was the taste that mattered. At the end of the meal he said he had not enjoyed such a good Sunday dinner since his mother had died. She felt such a glow of pleasure and gratitude that she hardly noticed when he took her father away without explaining why or where they were going.

It was not until the dishes had been washed that she realized she had been flattered into releasing her father without asking questions. Ramsay was a clever man. She did not blame him, only her own vanity and gullibility. Her anger returned.

'Come on!' she snapped at the children. 'We're going for a walk.'

'Mam!' They were horrified. 'Do we have to?'

She forced them into wellingtons, coats and gloves, knowing it to be an exercise in masochism because they would moan and whine all the time they were out. Let them. It would suit her mood. Jim was settled in a chair in front of the fire watching football on the television, and irritated her beyond reason. Ramsay might be a conceited, deceiving bastard, she thought, but she could not imagine him stretched in a chair like that, turning pink from the heat, his mouth wide open in the beginning of a snore. 'You could do with some exercise too,' she said and poked Jim viciously in the stomach. But he took no notice of her and turned back to the game.

It was a damp, raw day. A wet mist had blown in from the sea and immediately covered their clothes and hair with fine droplets of moisture. The smoke from the coal fires hung in the valley, so the fog was dirty and grey.

'Mam,' Andrew said. The word drawled into a wail of complaint. 'It's raining.'

'You're not sugar,' she said. 'You'll not melt.'

'Can't we take the car and go to Whitley Bay?'

For a moment she was tempted. The children, she knew, were seduced by the amusement arcades, the prospect of ice cream or fizzy drinks in a café, but she liked the seaside town in the winter. She liked the long empty sweep of the promenade, the monstrous shapes of the Spanish city fairground looming out of the mist and the sound of the foghorn on the buoy at the mouth of the Tyne. Later, she wished she had listened to them and taken the car into the town where the coloured neon lights shone into the gloom.

'No,' she said. 'We'll go for a walk. The fresh air will do us good.' She took their hands and dragged them along so they were almost running.

She wanted to get away from the village and took them along one of the lanes that led to the coast. They passed the old mill, where the Wilcoxes lived, and as always she looked in, fascinated by the style of the furniture, their imagined sophistication. But although both cars were in the drive, there was no sign of life and she presumed that they were all in the kitchen at the back of the house. Perhaps they were eating a late Sunday lunch.

I bet Hannah Wilcox doesn't cook soggy vegetables, Patty thought. I bet her gravy isn't lumpy.

She longed, for once, to do something well.

Out of Heppleburn the lane became narrow, and the grass verge where Patty made the children walk was sodden. On one side of the lane was a wood and the brown leaves dripped over the road and blocked out the light. The few cars that passed them were already using headlights and were identical dark shadows camouflaged by mist. On the other side, between the grass verge and the hedge, was a ditch. Patty knew that Andrew was attracted by it. Water of any kind acted like a magnet. She held his arm firmly and pulled him away. The hedge had lost most of its leaves and they could look through it into a muddy field where turnips were growing.

'How much further?' Jennifer asked. She had begun to drag her feet. Her trousers and anorak were splashed and stained.

'Not much further,' Patty said, beginning to relent. She felt better for being out of the house and the children had surprised her by being good. She wanted to be home when her father arrived. The thought that Ramsay might come in again excited her. 'Up to the bend in the road, then we'll turn back.'

Several hundred yards further on the road curved suddenly. There was a gap in the hedge there and a pull-in for tractors to get into the field. The ditch disappeared into a culvert, and emerged again. Andrew was fascinated by it and edged closer and closer.

They were about to turn back and cross the road to face the oncoming traffic when Andrew, with a splash of muddy water, fell in. Patty had released her grip on him for an instant to take Jennifer's hand to cross the road. He had been leaning forward, trying to reach the hedge, when the bank collapsed and he slid down, the heels of his wellingtons gouging deep grooves in the mud. He sat in the water at the bottom, half crying and half laughing while Patty looked on. There was an inevitability about the scene which made her relatively calm and she felt exasperation rather than anger.

'Stand up,' she said, 'and give me your hand. I'll pull you out.'

He slithered to his feet and she reached out to help him. She was leaning over to haul him up by the sleeves of his drenched and slimy anorak when her attention was attracted to the ditch near to the entrance into the field. She stared with disbelief. Andrew was too concerned with his own drama to notice that anything was wrong.

'Come on, Mam,' he said, enjoying himself, 'before I get stuck.'

She pulled the boy out and stood him on the road. She realized that she must be filthy.

'Go on,' she said. 'Start walking back. Both of you. Quickly or you'll catch your death of cold.'

Excited by the adventure the children started back towards the village, Andrew telling with great detail the horror of his slide into the abyss. Patty watched them go, then walked on a few paces. The track into the field was churned by tractor tyres. She forced herself to stare once more into the ditch. There, its hair matted and floating to the surface like weed, its head completely submerged by water, lay the body of a man. It lay face down and the shoulders and buttocks broke the surface of the water. Patty could not see the face but she recognized the clothes. No one else in the village had such a smart leather jacket, or wore jeans with an expensive label on the back pocket. The body belonged to Paul Wilcox. Saying nothing she hurried after Andrew and Jennifer.

The walk home was a nightmare. She was overwhelmed by a panic so intense that she could hardly move. It was not that she imagined a murderer lurking behind every hedge or tree. It was that suddenly the world was a dangerous and irrational place. It was the same feeling of panic she had experienced when she had left home for the first time to go to college in the south. She had felt then that she could trust no one. The prosperous town near to the college was so alien that she felt that houses, streets, might change or disappear overnight. Every time she went out she was frightened of getting lost. Now she had the same feeling of extreme insecurity. Harold Medburn's death had provoked a different reaction. That was ritualized, a sort of game. There was nothing playful about the body lying face down in the ditch. It went against everything she had ever known. She felt the laws of nature had been reversed. She walked on in a dream and only Andrew's increasingly loud complaints that he was cold and wet kept her sane.

The quickest way back was past the old mill, so she went that way though she wished she could avoid it. Her eyes were drawn to the window. Hannah Wilcox sat on a rocking chair there with Elizabeth on her knee. She was holding a book for the child but her eyes were on the horizon, as if she were waiting for someone to appear outside. Patty hurried past. She was terrified that the woman might come into the garden and ask if Patty had seen her husband. Ramsay had to be told first. He was a professional. He would know how to break such devastating news.

When they arrived home Ramsay's car was parked in the road outside the house. Patty opened the door and sent the children upstairs to bathe. The men must have just come in because they were still wearing coats. Her father was talking. He seemed in a jubilant, almost drunken mood. She wanted to tell Ramsay about Paul Wilcox but her father would not stop talking and although she opened her mouth no words would come out. It was Jim who noticed how upset she was. The others saw her only as a clown, covered with mud. It was Jim who interrupted Jack Robson.

'Patty,' he said. 'What is it?'

'Paul Wilcox is dead,' she said. 'I found his body. By the side of the lane that leads to the coast past the old mill.'

She was aware of the sudden silence, of the carefully controlled disbelief.

'Was it a road accident?' Jim asked and she realized that he at least believed her. That had never occurred to her and she felt a spasm of relief. 'Perhaps it was,' she said. 'Perhaps it was a hit and run accident. He was in the ditch.'

Then Ramsay was sitting beside her on the settee, asking her questions. In his gentle, intimate voice he probed through her panic, demanded her attention. Where exactly was the body? Had she told anyone else about it? Did she pass anyone on the road? Was there perhaps a car that she recognized?

She answered as calmly as she could, because she knew that was what he wanted and she wanted to please him. Then he was gone and she burst into tears. Upstairs the children were shouting and splashing in the bath and the sound of their laughter echoed around the house.

The news of Paul Wilcox's death did nothing to diminish Jack Robson's good humour. If anything it made him more excited. If it were murder, he said, there would be no reason to keep Kitty Medburn in custody. The police would have to release her immediately. There couldn't after all be two murderers in a village the size of Heppleburn.

His lack of sensitivity increased Patty's feeling of unreality. It was out of character. Her father seemed a different sort of man. He's obsessed by that woman, she thought. Perhaps she's a witch after all and she's cast a spell on him. Then she remembered what the vicar had said about the friendship being founded on fantasy. He's turned her into a saint, she thought, or an angel. He's going to be disappointed when he realizes she's an ordinary woman, like me. She's not a witch. But she's not an angel either.

Eventually, to their relief, Jack fell asleep, almost in mid-sentence.

The incident in the school house and the excitement of his meeting with Kitty Medburn had exhausted him. Patty and Jim waited in silence for Ramsay's return.

It was nine o'clock when the policeman finally knocked at the door. The house was quiet. The children were in bed and Jack was still sleeping. Jim sat beside her and felt awkward because there was nothing to do to help. She would not talk to him. She felt that by an effort of will she could arrange the facts so that Paul Wilcox had not been killed after all. She could persuade herself that she had made a mistake. She had seen not Paul Wilcox but a bundle of rags that had been dumped in the ditch. And if he were dead, it might be possible to convince herself that there had been an accident. He had been knocked down by a frightened driver on the grey, badly lit road. She heard the knock at the door but was so tense with the strain of these thoughts that she could not move. Jim let Ramsay into the house and the policeman walked straight into the living room as if he were a family friend.

'I can't stay long,' he said in a low voice. He seemed eager not to wake Jack. 'As you can imagine there's a lot to do.'

'So it was Paul Wilcox?' Patty said. She had known all along that it was.

Ramsay nodded.

'Was there anything I should have done?' Patty said. 'Perhaps I should have tried to revive him. But I thought perhaps I shouldn't touch him.'

And I couldn't have done it, she thought. I couldn't have got any closer to him. I would have been ill.

'No,' Ramsay said firmly. 'There was nothing you could have done.'

He began to leave the room when suddenly Jack woke up with a start, like a character in a badly written situation comedy. It was so like comic acting that Patty wondered if he had been asleep at all.

'What's going on?' he said. 'What happened?'

'Paul Wilcox is dead,' she said.

'You told me that earlier,' he said. 'But how did he die? Was it a car accident? Or was he murdered?'

'Mr Wilcox was murdered,' Ramsay said reluctantly. She thought he was embarrassed as if there was something he had failed to tell them. 'It's too early to be certain, but it seems that he was strangled.'

'There you are!' Jack struggled out of his chair. He had lost all trace of fatigue. 'You'll have to let Kitty go now.' He was already planning her return home. He would get champagne, the real stuff. He had never in his life drunk champagne.

Ramsay was silent for a moment, as if considering how much to say.

'I'm sorry,' he said. 'It's too late for that.'

'What do you mean?' Jack was puzzled. 'You know that she can't have killed Paul Wilcox so it's obvious that Kitty isn't the murderer.'

'Oh yes,' Ramsay said. 'That's obvious now. I don't believe Mrs Medburn killed her husband.'

'Well!' Jack was beginning to get angry. 'When are you going to let her go?'

'I'm sorry,' Ramsay repeated. 'I've got some terrible news for you.' He hesitated. 'Mrs Medburn's dead. She committed suicide this afternoon. She hanged herself.'

'Why?' Jack cried. 'I told her I'd get her out. Why didn't she trust me?'

He turned on Ramsay. 'You killed her. If you'd let her go earlier she'd still be alive.'

'No,' Ramsay said. 'She was never frightened of captivity.'

'Then what was going on? What were they doing to her in that place?'

'Nothing.' Ramsay spoke gently. 'She left a note for you. Perhaps you'll understand then. She was afraid, I think, of being released.'

Chapter Nine

After Kitty Medburn's suicide Ramsay, according to his colleagues lost all sense of proportion. He spent all day and most of the night in Heppleburn and if he slept at all it was in the chair in his office.

'It's the divorce,' Hunter said. 'It's finally caught up with him. That and guilt because the old lady killed herself.'

Hunter, who had always wanted an inspector's salary, watched Ramsay's slow disintegration with satisfaction, and took as little part as possible in the inquiry. So Ramsay ran the investigation almost alone and made up his own rules as he went along. He felt he had nothing to lose.

Monday, the day after the second murder, Angela Brayshaw received the letter for which she had been waiting. It had been posted on the preceding Thursday and had been unaccountably delayed in the post. If it had arrived on time, she thought, she would have been saved a troublesome and unpleasant weekend. The letter was from Harold Medburn's solicitors and informed her that she was the sole beneficiary of his estate. She wondered briefly how her mother would take the news.

Jim had offered to stay at home with Patty. She was touched by his concern but sent him to work. She preferred to be alone. Besides, she felt that only the normal domestic routine would prevent her from dissolving into panic. There was nothing to prevent her following the usual pattern. Jack had insisted on going home the night before. They were worried about him – he seemed so blank and withdrawn – and they had not wanted to let him go, but Patty could understand that he needed to be alone and it was a relief to have him out of the house. So she tried to put the horror of the day before from her mind. Surprisingly she had dreamed not about Paul Wilcox, but about Ramsay. In normal times she might have been concerned by this obsession with a stranger, by the dreams, the excitement. She always considered herself happily married and avoided contacts which might make her dissatisfied with Jim. Now, with her security shattered anything seemed possible and she clung to the image of Ramsay, as if he alone could make her happy again. From the beginning she had been attracted by him. It seemed now he was the only man strong enough to set her world to rights.

That morning she got up a little early. She was calmer and more efficient than she might otherwise have been on a Monday. She even had time to wash the breakfast dishes and make the beds before walking the children to school. They too were quiet and subdued.

The playground was crowded with parents. Even the careless mothers, the slatterns, who usually stood on the doorstep unwashed and undressed, to wave their children out alone, were there this morning. They would have heard of the murder. Patty was aware of stares and whispers. They would have heard too that she had found the body. Patty stood alone and waited until Andrew and Jennifer were safely in the school.

When she got home Ramsay was sitting in his car outside her house. He saw her approaching and got out to stand on the pavement. He might have been a lover impatient to take her into his arms. It would have been warmer, she thought, to wait in the car. The fog had lasted all night, but now, as she walked down the road towards him the sun broke through the mist. It was a hazy globe above his head.

'I need to talk to you,' he said.

'One of your men came last night and took a statement.'

She could not make polite conversation with him; She wanted to be honest but she was not sure what he wanted. It would be easier if he went, then she could resume the ritual of the day.

'I know,' he said. 'It's not that. I need your help.'

'Do you want to come in?'

'No,' he said. 'I'll take you out. Where shall we go?'

She thought of the previous day, of the children's appeal: can't we take the car and go to Whitley Bay? 'Let's go to Whitley,' she said. It represented safety, the time before the walk up the gloomy lane, the possibility of fun.

'Why not?' he said.

It was a big car and he seemed to drive off very fast. There was something reckless and exhilarating about driving to the coast beside an attractive man and she thought again that the old rules of her life no longer applied. He pushed in a cassette which played loud music – opera, she thought. It was hot in the car and she found it hard to breathe. He smelled of pipe tobacco and leather.

A scattering of old ladies were walking dogs on the links, but the beach was almost empty. The mist had disappeared and there was a soft breeze from the southwest. It was like an early spring day. He opened the car door for her with a flourish and they walked along the promenade towards Cullercoats. On the other side of the road there were chip shops, amusement arcades. In the sunshine they seemed less sleazy and dismal than usual. They were jolly, with a fifties innocence. The light was clear and reflected on the wet, ridged sand and the retreating tide. Everything was clean and bright. She saw it all very sharply.

He ran across the road to buy her an ice cream and returned with a huge multi-coloured cornet. It seemed to her a frivolous gesture. She felt the morning had a great significance and wished he would take it more seriously.

'Aren't you busy?' she said. She thought he was being irresponsible. Surely he should be working. There was a murderer in Heppleburn and he was enjoying a jaunt to the seaside. She did not recognize his desperation.

'I thought you would like ice cream,' he said. 'But perhaps you would have preferred the candy floss.'

She held the ice cream awkwardly. It dribbled down the cone and onto her fingers. 'I don't want to take up your time,' she said. She wanted him to say that although his time was valuable he would give it to her.

'It helps me to get away from it for a while,' he said. 'I've not had much sleep.'

They walked on until they came to a seat looking out over the beach, and sat there. A woman in jeans and sweater was pushing an old lady in a wheelchair along the promenade. They were laughing together over some joke.

'How can I help you?' Patty asked. It was what he had been waiting for and he answered immediately.

'Give me your time,' he said, 'and your local knowledge. Listen to what's going on in the village and tell me what you find out. I was sure Kitty Medburn killed her husband. Of course I was wrong and I have to start from the beginning again. You and your father discovered more by poking around the village than I ever will. I had a long talk to Jack on Saturday night and I was impressed. Jack's no good to me now. He's distraught. He'll blame himself for Kitty's death. Besides, he's lost his incentive. He doesn't care who the murderer is.'

'I've no incentive,' she said.

'But you'll help,' he said, smiling at her. 'You *will* help.'

'I'm not easily bribed,' she said, to give herself time to think. 'I'll want more than an ice cream cornet.' She knew she would do anything he asked her.

'You'll have your village back,' he said. 'When the murderer's found, it'll belong to you again.'

She looked up suddenly, amazed and flattered because he understood so well. 'What do you want me to do?'

Later she thought he must have enchanted her because she agreed so readily to his plans. Perhaps the shock of finding Paul Wilcox's body had left her weak and impressionable. Perhaps it was because she had been attracted to him from the first time they met, in her front room, after Medburn's murder. She knew she was being manipulated but could do nothing about it. He smiled at her, as if she had lived up to all his expectations.

'What you've been doing all along,' he said. 'Listen. You're a good listener. You persuaded Angela Brayshaw to talk to you about

Harold Medburn. Talk to her again. Medburn left her all his money in his will. Did she tell you that?'

'No,' she said. 'She didn't mention it. Perhaps Harold hadn't told her that he was making a will in her favour.'

'Perhaps. Or perhaps she's cleverer than we realize.' He turned away from her and she quickly dropped the remainder of the ice cream into a litter bin and wiped her face with a handkerchief.

'Did your father tell you that Medburn was drugged before he died?' he asked.

'It was in the papers,' she said.

'He was drugged with Heminevrin, a medicine used in the care of old people. It's a controlled drug. I need to know who would have access to it.'

'Angela Brayshaw's mother runs an old people's home.'

'I know,' he said. 'I've been there. She's giving nothing away.'

'Paul Wilcox used to be a nurse,' she said, trying to be helpful.

'Did he? That's hardly relevant now.'

'Should you be telling me all this?' Patty said helplessly. It seemed a terrible responsibility. 'Isn't it confidential? It doesn't seem right to discuss the case with me.'

'I trust you,' he said. It sounded better than confessing that he was making up his own rules for the investigation. 'I need a result soon. The press is already having a field day about Kitty's suicide. They're blaming the police for her death of course. They have a point. I made a mistake. I should never have arrested her.'

She wanted to console him, to tell him that she did not blame him, but he wanted more than that. 'I'll do what I can,' she said. 'I don't think I can be much use.'

She hesitated. 'Have you been to see Hannah Wilcox?'

'Yes,' he said.

'I suppose she'll be going home to her parents.'

'No,' he said. 'I don't think so. She told me she wanted to stay at the old mill. She thought it would be better for the children.'

'But she must be so lonely!' Patty cried.

'Perhaps you should visit her,' the policeman suggested smoothly.

'She needs friends now. And she'll probably find it easier to talk to you than me.'

'You want me to interview her for you?'

'Of course not,' he said. The disapproval was assumed. 'Not that. But if you did discover anything relevant to the inquiry you'd have a duty to tell me.'

'Yes,' she said. 'I see.' She did not have the strength to argue with him, but realized that she had been used again. She had been trapped, not this time by flattering words, but by a ride in a fast car, the sunshine and his attention. It made no difference to how she felt about him. They went back to Heppleburn in silence.

Early the next afternoon Patty called at the old mill. Hannah was alone. Joe was at school and Lizzie, the baby, was upstairs in bed. Hannah was sitting in the window, in the same chair as when Patty had seen her on the day of Paul's death. She must have seen Patty walking through the trees but she did not move. Perhaps she hoped Patty would see her lack of response as rejection and turn away. But Patty continued up the gravel path and knocked at the back door. There was a long pause and she could hear the burn beyond the garden. There was no sound within the house and she was about to go away when the door opened. Hannah was flushed and her eyes were very bright as if she were feverish.

'Come in,' she said quickly. All her movements were violent and jerky. 'Do come in.'

'I'm sorry,' Patty said. 'Perhaps I shouldn't interfere. But I thought there might be something I could do.'

Patty knew she would never endure even a lesser crisis alone, in a strange part of the country without the support of her family and friends. Hannah seemed not to be listening. Throughout the conversation she was restless, nervous, and Patty had the impression that this was only an intensification of her usual state.

'If you'd prefer to be alone,' Patty said, 'just tell me and I'll go away.'

'No,' Hannah said. 'It was kind of you to come. I must seem

very rude.' She opened the door wide. 'Would you like some tea? I expect you would.'

She switched taps full on and filled a kettle. There was a pile of dishes in the sink and she began to wash two mugs, then gave up and took clean ones from hooks on the wall. She banged open cupboards and drawers with a random frenzy.

'I don't know where Paul put the tea,' she said helplessly. 'I'm not here much and he saw to all that.'

Patty found the tea in a caddy on the work top. There was milk in the fridge. She had never been in the old mill and was reassured by the domestic clutter. Hannah Wilcox was not very different from her after all.

They took the tea into the long living room. It smelled fusty, of stale smoke, and Patty wished she could open a window. The Sunday papers were still lying open on a coffee table. There was a dirty mug and a plate with a half-eaten piece of toast on the window sill. Hannah kicked open the door of a big wood-burning stove and threw on more logs.

'I feel so cold,' she said. 'I can't seem to get warm.'

'It'll be the shock.'

'I suppose it is.' Hannah looked at Patty. 'You found his body, didn't you? That must have been a shock too.' She walked backwards and forwards in front of the stove then sat on the hearth rug and stared at Patty, waiting for an answer.

'It was.'

'Did you know Paul well?'

'Not well. Only through the Parents' Association. But I liked him. I thought he was brave. It can't have been easy for him staying at home with the children. My husband would never manage it.'

'No, I never realized how hard he found it, not until it was too late.' Hannah paused. 'Would you mind if I talked to you about him? I've no-one else to talk to. My mother wants to come and look after me but I can't stand the thought of anyone staying in the house. I haven't seen anyone since the policewoman went. Except the children. Mrs Irving will pick Joe up from school for me but she won't stay.'

'Of course,' Patty said. She remembered that Ramsay had said she was a good listener. It was nice, she thought bitterly, to be considered good at something.

Hannah was curled up on the rug. She seemed to have shrunk, to be no bigger than a child. She wore large round spectacles which covered most of her face. She was very dark – dark-haired, olive-skinned, exotic. Then she jumped up and lit a cigarette. Patty wished she would sit still.

'Paul wanted me to give up smoking,' she said, 'but I could never manage it.' She seemed to Patty to have enormous energy. Patty thought she would always be dissatisfied, looking forward to new plans, a new challenge.

'Did you know Paul had a lover?' she asked suddenly. Patty was shocked, a little embarrassed.

'No,' she said awkwardly, 'I had no idea. He always seemed so happy.' It seemed tactless to mention that Jack had seen Paul and Angela together on the night of the bonfire.

'He thought I didn't know,' Hannah said, and she wandered off again to fetch an ashtray.

'But you found out?'

'I guessed,' she said. 'Paul was an innocent. I could tell he was guilty about something. Then I thought it must be over.'

'You didn't ask him?' Patty imagined the scenes there would be in their house if she suspected Jim of infidelity. She would never pretend that nothing was wrong. There would be thrown plates, shouting, tears.

'No,' Hannah said. 'I didn't ask him. Perhaps I didn't want to know. It would have been a reflection on our marriage. I couldn't afford to give it any more time.' She looked at Patty with dry, angry eyes. 'Now I would give all the time in the world to have him back.'

She began to pace again and to talk, as if movement and speech were some relief.

'He'd written poetry to her,' Hannah said. 'I never found out until the morning he died. He'd written poetry to her and the cow had given the poems to Harold Medburn. Medburn blackmailed

Paul. He was frightened that I'd find out, that I might leave him, as if I hadn't in a way left him already.'

'When did you find out about this?'

'The morning of the day he died. Sunday morning.' She began to speak more quickly, a stream of words, part confession of her own responsibility, part a terrible reliving of the hours and days before her husband's death.

'We all went to the bonfire on the recreation ground on Saturday evening,' she said. 'I could tell that something had been worrying him all day. He took the children to the swings in the afternoon and came home in a furious temper. We had a row about the bonfire. He didn't want to come with us, but I persuaded him. It would be fun, I said. The children would enjoy it. We went to the recreation ground together but early in the evening he disappeared. He didn't tell me he was going home or that he was feeling ill. He just vanished. I didn't think too much of it. He was in a bad mood and wanted to be on his own. I expected him to be at home when we returned, but the house was empty. I started to be worried, but I got the children ready for bed, and soon after he came in. He was in a terrible state. He poured himself a drink and his hands were shaking so much that he spilled it. I asked him to tell me what was the matter. Whatever it was, we could sort it out together. He said he'd done something terrible, despicable. I told him I didn't care and I'd love him just the same. But he wouldn't talk to me. He went straight to bed and I could feel him lying beside me, rigid and wide awake. He was cold. He'd had a shock too, you see.

'In the middle of the night he thought I was asleep. He got out of bed and came downstairs. I was worried and followed him down. I didn't mean to pry on him, but I thought he'd feel better if he could share whatever was troubling him. He was standing here in front of the stove, holding a pile of papers. I thought they were letters. He was tearing them into little pieces and throwing them on the fire.' She paused for breath, took off her glasses and rubbed them with the hem of her jersey. Without her spectacles Patty could see that the skin around her eyes was tight and strained. 'I thought he would be angry,' she continued, 'because I'd followed him. I would have been. But I think he was glad. It showed at least that I cared. We sat up all night talking. He told me what had happened.'

Hannah returned to the hearth rug and kneeled in front of the stove.

'While he was at the swings on the Saturday afternoon he met Angela Brayshaw,' she said. 'That was the woman with whom he'd been having an affair. She taunted him. She practically admitted that she had given his letters and poems to Harold Medburn. It must have been a great relief to Paul when Medburn died, but he was worried that the poems were still in the school house and that someone else might find them. He seems to have been completely irrational about it. While we were at the bonfire, he was desperate and decided to go to look for them. He broke into the school house through a kitchen window and had just found them when your father surprised him.'

Hannah looked apologetically at Patty. 'He was frightened,' she said. 'He didn't mean to hit Mr Robson so hard. Then he was terrified in case he had killed him.'

'But he didn't stop,' Patty said, 'to see if my father needed help.'

'No,' said Hannah. 'But he heard someone else outside and realized your father wouldn't be left alone.'

'Did he see who that was?' Patty asked.

'I think he might have done.' Hannah thought, an intense effort to remember exactly. 'Yes, he must have done. He said he looked out of the window, realized your father would be in safe hands and ran away, climbing out through the kitchen again. Of course he felt dreadful about what happened and was still afraid that he might have killed Mr Robson until Sunday morning when we heard he'd just had a nasty bump on the head. That's why he was so upset on Saturday night.'

'Did he tell you,' Patty asked, 'who else he saw? Who was in the school house that night?'

'I don't know,' said Hannah. 'Is it important?'

Patty did not answer directly.

'He didn't rig up a dummy, dressed as a witch, to frighten my father away?'

'Of course not. There was no need. Your father was unconscious.' She lit another cigarette. 'What is all this about?'

'My father was looking into Harold Medburn's death,' Patty said. 'I know it sounds ridiculous, but Kitty Medburn was an old friend of his and he was convinced that she was innocent. He'd been asking a lot of awkward questions in the village – Paul wasn't the only person threatened by blackmail. When he regained consciousness there was a dummy dressed as a witch hanging from the kitchen ceiling and a message telling him to mind his own business. It was an attempt, you see, to frighten him off. I think Dad was followed from the bonfire by Harold Medburn's murderer. Don't you see, if Paul saw whoever it was, that might explain why he had to die.'

'Yes,' Hannah said. 'I see.' She stood up. She was wearing stretch jeans and a long loose pullover. There was no trace of the smart controlled businesswoman. 'Why are you here?' she asked. 'Did your father send you?'

'No,' Patty said. 'The policeman, Ramsay, thought you might need a friend.'

'Did he tell you what questions to ask?'

'Not exactly.' Patty was impressed by Hannah's intelligence and thought she deserved honesty. 'He thought you might find it easier to talk to me. He's determined to find out who killed your husband. He's prepared to use unorthodox means.'

'Good!' For the first time in the conversation Hannah seemed to find a sort of peace. 'Well, perhaps he was right. I do find it easier to talk to you. Do you need to ask me any more questions?'

'What happened on Sunday morning?'

'We all had a long, late breakfast together,' Hannah said. 'It was lovely. Like a new beginning. All the pretence was gone. We were talking about the future. Paul said he was longing to go back to work. We decided to go into the possibility of employing a nanny. Then I went to the paper shop to see if there was any news of Mr Robson. That's when I heard he was okay and staying with you.'

'Did you notice anything unusual on the way out?'

'No,' she said. 'The police asked me that, I think there may have been a car parked in the lane, but I can't remember anything about it, not even the colour. I hadn't put in my contact lenses and I wasn't wearing specs, so I was nearly blind.'

'When did Paul go out?'

'At about mid-day. We'd decided to eat in the evening. He said he wanted some exercise. I could understand that. It had been a traumatic evening.'

'You don't think he had arranged to meet someone?'

'No,' she said. 'I'm sure not.' She drew on the cigarette. 'He could have made a telephone call while I was at the paper shop, but he would have told me. I explained. We had decided there would be no more pretence. Besides, he was a hopeless liar. I would have known; I'm sure it was a spur of the moment decision.'

'I see.' Patty hesitated. She felt awkward. 'Paul was a nurse, wasn't he, before he stopped working?'

'Yes,' Hannah said. 'He was a psychiatric nurse. He worked in a special unit for alcoholics.'

'Does he still have friends there?'

'A few. Why? Is it important?'

'Harold Medburn was doped with a drug called Heminevrin before he was murdered. I'm trying to find out who would have had access to it.'

'But Paul couldn't have murdered Harold Medburn!'

'I have to ask,' Patty said, 'if you want to find out the truth. Are you sure you really want to know?'

'Yes.' Hannah looked at her intensely, her dark eyes magnified by the strong glasses. 'You will do your best, won't you? Whatever you find out.'

'Of course,' Patty said. It was a similar responsibility to her commitment to Ramsay.

She looked at her watch. It was time to fetch the children. As she left the old mill she walked past the window. Hannah was back in the rocking chair, her arms around her knees, staring out towards the road.

It seemed to Patty that Ramsay spent all his time that week in the village. Wherever she went in Heppleburn she saw his car, his distinctive back at doorsteps or disappearing round corners. Everyone was talking about him. In the playground she stood apart and listened to the mothers talking, because Ramsay had said she was good at listening. He's bewitched me, she thought, in the same way as Kitty Medburn bewitched my father. They speculated about Ramsay's background and marital status and through listening to them she gathered that he was trying to find out who had taken the witch's costume from the pram on the night of the bonfire. He or his men must have spoken to everyone who was on the recreation ground that night. Rumour had it that these investigations had so far proved unsuccessful. Many people admitted to having seen the confrontation between Matthew Carpenter and the boys, but then there had been so many distractions – the excitement of the fire and the noise and colour of the fireworks – that the costume was forgotten. The pram had been pushed into the shadow and no one saw it again until the boys fetched it to take it home. They realized that the costume was missing, but thought it had been confiscated by Matthew Carpenter. Despite his persistence Ramsay seemed to have got no further.

That Tuesday afternoon the policeman was back at the school. His car was parked in the playground and Patty could see his dark head through the staff room window. She waited a long time for him to emerge. She wanted to share the information given to her by Hannah. She thought he would be pleased. But there was no sign of the inspector leaving the school. All the other parents and children disappeared, but Matthew Carpenter, Irene Hunt and Stephen Ramsay remained inside. Eventually Andrew and Jennifer became so cold and fractious that she left without talking to him. It would be impossible to have a serious discussion with the children in that mood.

On the way home she called at her father's house. She was worried about his continued depression, but she felt too that she needed his support. She had some vague hope that he would have come to terms with Kitty's death and she would be able to share with him Hannah's information. The hope was not realized. When Jack Robson came to the door he was clean and tidily dressed. He was polite, thanked her for calling and said he was fine, but he did not invite them in and made it clear that he wanted them to go. Nothing she could say would console him.

Jack stood at his window and watched them go with relief. He could not bear his daughter's pity. He walked back to the mantelshelf and took down the note which Kitty Medburn had written before hanging herself from a curtain rail in the shower room at the remand centre.

He knew the words by heart but read them again.

'I'm sorry, Jack,' it said. 'I could never live up to your dreams.'

Chapter Ten

Ramsay was haunted by a growing desperation and isolation. His colleagues seemed to have distanced themselves from him. He, after all, had taken the decision to arrest Kitty Medburn and there would be an inquiry into her suicide. And now, instead of covering his back, of following police procedure to the letter, he had begun to work in a way that was even more idiosyncratic and unorthodox. Those who were concerned about their own careers made their disapproval of his methods clear. It was a bad thing to be associated with failure.

In the police station at Otterbridge, in the canteen and corridors people whispered and waited for his downfall. Hunter seemed to grow in influence and stature.

Ramsay knew that others considered him a failure but was too proud, too clear-sighted about past achievements to accept their judgement. It was all added pressure though at a time in an inquiry which was always most difficult. He knew that a positive result was possible, but could not even guess who the murderer was. More than usual he felt that this case was a battle for survival. He was convinced that the answer lay in Heppleburn and was always drawn back to the school. He had become fascinated, almost obsessed, with the personality of the headmaster. There, with wilful and inconsistent autocracy, Harold Medburn had ruled. There he had been murdered. Although he had no evidence Ramsay felt that the death of Paul Wilcox was almost an irrelevance. Wilcox was a weak and ineffective man who would have no natural enemies. Unless it was the work of a lunatic, his death was an attempt by the murderer to cover his tracks. Ramsay thought that the murderer too was becoming desperate.

Medburn had been different, Ramsay thought as he parked his car in the playground, avoiding a crocodile of children returning from a nature walk. Medburn had been larger than life, a worthy victim of murder. At times, when he was almost faint with sleeplessness, he could imagine the headmaster taunting and teasing him. He knew that to be ridiculous, but the personality of the victim, his own pride and his guilt at Kitty's suicide made this case special. He was determined to get a result.

Ramsay knew that his visits to the school had begun to irritate the staff, and as he approached the building he thought he could already sense their hostility. Jack Robson was seldom there now. Since Kitty's death he seemed only to go to the school early in the morning and last thing at night. Occasionally Ramsay did meet him and then he was withdrawn and resentful.

There had been changes in the school. The vicar's wife had come in as supply teacher to take Miss Hunt's class while she was acting head teacher and the secretary, an elderly lady, had resigned with accusations and floods of tears. She had seemed to think that death, like the measles, was contagious and she could not stay there without being affected. Perhaps she was right, thought Ramsay, remembering Kitty Medburn and Paul Wilcox.

Ramsay went into the school and along the corridor to Matthew Carpenter's room. He knew his way round now. He knocked at the door and the teacher came into the corridor to speak to him. As if I'm infectious too, Ramsay thought, and the children might catch something from me. Inside the children were painting.

'Yes Inspector,' Matthew said. 'Can I help you?'

'Just a few more questions.' In interview the young man had always been pleasant and polite. He had already answered Ramsay's questions about the bonfire, the children's attempts to dress the guy as a witch. But now Ramsay wanted to ask about the rumours that Matthew had been threatened by Medburn with dismissal. He wondered if Carpenter would be so eager to discuss that.

'Could you wait for five minutes?' Matthew asked. 'The children will be going home then and we can talk in peace.'

Ramsay nodded and prowled along the corridor, as if by being in the building, by walking as the headmaster had done, he would receive some inspiration about who had hated the man so much to kill him and then to dress him up in such a grotesque and undignified way. He felt he had wasted time. He had believed so strongly that Kitty had killed her husband that he had not taken sufficient notice of the other people involved while they were still shocked by Medburn's death and might have given something away. The fingerprint and forensic tests had not helped. All the fingerprints in the school belonged to people who had a reason to be there and that only reinforced his theory that the murderer was connected with the school.

A bell rang and the children pushed into the corridor, then ran into the playground. In Matthew's classroom the two men sat on children's desks. Ramsay began his questions gently, retracing old ground about the bonfire, asking for the names and addresses of the children who were there. Then he began to inquire about Matthew's relationship with Medburn.

'You didn't get on with Mr Medburn, did you?' Ramsay asked.

'We had different ideas about teaching.'

'But he was a headmaster and you had just qualified so he was in a position to impose his ideas on you?'

'I suppose so.'

'Isn't it true that he didn't think much of you as a teacher?'

'I don't know,' Matthew had begun to stammer but he remained polite, quiet. 'Perhaps I wasn't as strong on discipline as he would have liked.'

'I've heard that he was going to get you the sack.'

'I don't know where you could have heard that.' Matthew's voice was louder and he was starting to lose control. 'You shouldn't listen to the parents' gossip.'

'But you've been happier here since Mr Medburn died?'

'Yes. If you've been talking in the village you'll know that I'm happier now. So are all the children.'

Without a pause Ramsay changed the subject of his questions. 'Were you drunk on the night of the Hallowe'en party?'

'Yes!' Matthew was almost shouting. 'I've admitted that before.'

'Why did you get drunk?'

'I don't know. I was lonely, unhappy, homesick. I missed my friends.'

'Do you lose control when you're drunk?'

'Not enough to commit murder.'

And although Matthew was angry and frightened, nothing Ramsay could say would shake him from that. Ramsay was surprised, throughout the interview, to see Irene Hunt looking in from the corridor, watchful and protective, as if she had coached the young man in what he would say and she wanted to ensure that he was word perfect. Her presence encouraged Ramsay in the belief that Carpenter had something to hide. He began to feel happier.

Ramsay had spoken to Miss Hunt earlier in the week and the memory of that interview remained with him in perfect detail. In her bungalow she had struck him as relaxed, human. He had liked her. At school she was quite different. She had seen him in the headmaster's office and had been as imperious and distant as Medburn himself. She had intimidated Ramsay with her sharp, honest intelligence and her refusal to compromise. And because she was a teacher of such an age and type, he admitted to himself later. As a child he had been terrified of a schoolmistress just like her. He'd had nightmares about her and dreamed she was an ogre.

Miss Hunt had answered his questions readily enough. She admitted to having been blackmailed, but then refused to give Ramsay her daughter's name and address.

'I can find it out,' he said, with a spasm of desperation and spite.

'I can't stop you doing that,' she said, cool and haughty, 'though I don't imagine it's as easy as you think. She changed her name of course when she was adopted and when she married, and she's moved several times. Even if you find her it's not important. I'll know that I've not betrayed her.'

Ramsay had set a constable to trace the daughter but without much urgency or hope of success. There had not yet been a result. Miss Hunt had been paying blackmail to Medburn for years. After that time it surely must have become a habit, a minor irritation and hardly a motive for murder. Besides, if she were to be believed she no longer had any reason to pay.

Out in the corridor Miss Hunt caught his eye and walked away. Matthew Carpenter stood up suddenly and began to clean the blackboard. The rubber was dusty and chalk was smeared across the blackboard, despite the young man's vigorous, almost frantic, actions. Ramsay watched with a growing joy. Carpenter was frightened. He knew he had to act carefully now. It was vital to show that the teacher had access to Heminevrin. He could not take Carpenter in on suspicion for questioning without that proof. He had done that to Kitty Medburn and his superiors would need evidence before they would allow it to happen again. They were too sensitive to criticism by the press.

'You live above a chemist's shop, don't you?' he asked.

Matthew looked round quickly and the blackboard rubber banged to the floor.

'Yes,' he said as he bent to pick it up.

'Is there any way into it from your flat?'

'No. I've got a separate entrance.'

'So there's no way you could get into the shop if it's closed?'

'Oh yes,' Matthew said. 'The pharmacist rented the flat to me on the condition that I keep an eye on the shop. It's been broken into a couple of times and sometimes the burglar alarm goes off by mistake. I've got a spare key.'

He seemed unaware that he was making any dramatic revelation and Ramsay's conviction that he was the murderer was shaken by Carpenter's frankness. The policeman felt he needed time for reflection. He was too involved in the case. He had spent too much time in the grey terraced streets of the village and the school on the hill. The seaside walk along the promenade with Patty Atkins seemed to have happened a long time ago.

While he was interviewing Matthew Carpenter, Ramsay saw Patty hovering in the playground and the children pulling at her coat, trying to persuade her to go. He thought at first she was waiting for her father, then remembered he had asked her to speak to Hannah Wilcox. He was so convinced that the answer to the murders lay in the school that he was sure she would have little information of value. He was touched, though, by the effort she had made. He remembered the walk along the seafront with pleasure, because it had been a break from the depression of Heppleburn and because she had not criticized him. He was so used to being alone on this case that her company had been comforting. As soon as the interview with Matthew was over he rushed out to see her, but she had gone. He stood in the empty playground in the dusk, feeling he had been deserted.

Because she felt that the information from Hannah Wilcox was so important, Patty left a message for Ramsay at Otterbridge police station. The policeman there was unpleasantly insistent that she should talk to him rather than to his superior, but she refused. She had the impression that he was sneering at Ramsay. She felt she owed a loyalty to Ramsay and besides, although she would not admit it to herself, she knew his response to her message would provide an excuse for them to meet.

They did meet, but almost by chance, the next day at lunch-time in the main street of the village. He still had not returned her call and she had been restless all morning. Perhaps she went to the post office in the hope of seeing him. She stood in the street and looked at the advertisements in the window. Mrs Mount was advertising for a care assistant to work in the nursing home. Angela must have told her already that she would not help there. Then she turned round and he was standing on the pavement beside her, apparently in a dream.

'I tried to see you,' she said. 'There's something I think you should know. Have you time to talk to me now?'

'Of course!' The preoccupation disappeared and the flattering manner returned as if at the flick of a switch. He can't help it, she thought.

'Can we get something to eat at the Northumberland Arms?' he asked. 'We can have lunch together and you can talk to me then.'

It'll be all round the village in an hour, she thought, that I've been to the pub with the good-looking policeman. She wondered briefly what her husband would think, but she nodded and followed him into the lounge bar. Jim would understand. She chose a table in a corner, furthest away from the bar, under a poster of last year's leek show. Ramsay would not want to be overheard. They ate beef sandwiches and drank lager while she told him about Hannah's discovery that Paul Wilcox too had been threatened by blackmail, that Wilcox had been in the school house on the night of the bonfire and that someone else had been there too.

Ramsay listened with great care. 'He didn't give her any idea who that was?'

Patty shook her head.

'So Angela Brayshaw was involved with Wilcox too,' Ramsay said. He was thinking aloud. 'She gets around, that woman, doesn't she? A regular little gold-digger. Your father saw them together but I couldn't see them as a couple.' He looked at Patty. 'Tell me a bit more about her.' He was asking out of interest. He was still committed to the theory that Matthew Carpenter was involved with both murders.

'I don't know her very well,' Patty said, 'although her family have always lived in the village. Her dad died when she was young and apparently her mum used the insurance money to send her to a private school in Jesmond. Mrs Mount, her mother, was always a snob. She runs that private nursing home in the big house on the way to Morpeth and Angela helped there in the school holidays. She was never allowed out to parties or discos with us. Her mam thought we'd lead her astray. She had dreams of Angela going away to college, I think, but she didn't do very well at school. I remember talking to her once on the top of the bus into Newcastle when we were both sixteen. She wanted to work in a smart hairdresser's and do day release at the tech but Mrs Mount wouldn't have it. Too common for her only daughter. In the end Angela worked in the nursing home too.'

'I see,' he said, almost to himself. 'So she would have learned to lift there. She would have had to lift the old people into bed. Even though she's tiny she's quite strong.'

'You think she killed Harold Medburn for his money?' She was beyond caring now who had killed the headmaster. She just wanted the thing cleared up. 'There were all those rumours that she owed a lot to her mother and was having to work at the nursing home to pay it back. She always hated it there. She won't need to do that now.'

'No,' he said. 'I don't think that. But it's important to keep an open mind. Has she got a car?'

Patty nodded. 'Her mother bought it for her when she was separated. It's a Mini.'

'Go on,' he said. 'She started work at the nursing home. What happened then?'

'She married David Brayshaw,' Patty said. 'I never met him but everyone said he was far too nice for her.' Then, realizing how bitchy she must sound she added: 'Of course she was very pretty.'

'Was he local?'

'From Monkseaton I think. He was a trainee manager in a carpet factory. Angela gave up work in the nursing home as soon as she was married. Everyone knew she hated it. I don't think David was happy in his work either because he packed it all in when he left Angela.'

'When was that?'

'Soon after Claire was born. I don't know what he's doing now.'

'Thank you,' he said. 'You're a mine of information. Considering you don't know her very well.'

She realized he was laughing at her. 'I know it's all gossip,' she said.

'I was being serious,' he said. 'Really. You've been a great help.'

'There is something else,' she said.

'Yes?'

'Mrs Medburn used to help out at the old people's home. She'd go in at weekends to be in charge so that Angela's mother could get away. That's probably how Angela first met Harold.'

It seemed to him then that the whole village was in some way related and that the relationships were so tenuous, complex and informal that he would never untangle them. It occurred to him that he might be keen to accept Matthew Carpenter as the murderer because the teacher was an outsider and then the whole thing would be less complicated. As he had told Patty, it was important to keep an open mind.

'Will you talk to her?' he said. 'Just as a neighbour. Don't ask any specific questions, but if you come across anything suspicious let me know.'

'It's awkward,' she said. 'We're not particularly friendly.'

'But you'll try?' It was an echo of Hannah's plea for help. 'She'll not talk to me.'

'Yes,' she said. 'I'll try.' She was angry with herself because she agreed so easily. What was she? A mother to them all? The maternal responsibility of curing ills and making things better seemed an awful burden. But she was good at nothing else. It was all she could do.

It was odd to walk out of the dark, humid pub with its wood panels into broad daylight. It should have been evening, yet it was only half past one. There were two and a half hours before she needed to collect the children from school. She did not relish the thought of an interview with Angela Brayshaw and decided it would be better done now. She would get it over. But when she knocked on the glossy, green door it opened immediately and Angela stood on the threshold, her coat fastened, handbag and keys in her hand, obviously on her way out.

'What do you want?' she asked. She seemed more confident than on their previous encounter, looking at Patty with an amused superiority. Medburn's death must have shocked her, Patty thought, but she was getting over it now.

'Nothing special,' Patty said lamely. 'I just wondered how you were.'

'You came for a nose about Harold's money,' Angela said. 'I expect everyone in Heppleburn's talking about it. Well I can't give you any details. I don't know yet how much it'll be.'

'No,' Patty said. 'It wasn't that.' But she knew how unconvincing she must sound.

'I'm going out,' Angela said, 'to spend my money. I haven't time to gossip.' She set off quickly down the pavement, her keys still in her hand, towards the block of garages which were grouped at the end of the street. At the bottom of the road she turned and gave a cheerful almost pitying wave.

Later Patty was not sure what had prompted her to phone Burnside. Perhaps it was to prove to Angela Brayshaw that she could not be so easily dismissed. Perhaps it was because she thought Ramsey would be pleased. She looked up the number as soon as she got home, then dialled, without having time for nervousness or second thoughts.

The phone rang for a short time then a woman answered. Patty did not recognize the voice but knew it was not Mrs Mount.

'Hello,' she said. 'This is Mrs Atkins. I'm phoning about the care assistant's vacancy advertized in the post office window.'

Patty wondered before phoning whether she should use her real name, but decided that Mrs Mount would not recognize it. Even if she had heard that Jack had been asking questions in the village she would not know Patty's married name and was unlikely to connect the two.

'Just one moment.' The woman spoke in a strained, affected voice which she obviously saved for the telephone, because Patty heard her lapse into accent to say: 'Mrs Mount, there's a Mrs Atkins on the phone about the vacancy.' There was a whispered conversation then the woman said: 'Mrs Atkins? Could you come in for an interview this afternoon? Mrs Mount is available to see you today.'

'Yes,' Patty said, rather alarmed by the immediate result of the call. 'I'll be there in half an hour.'

It took her that long to make herself presentable. All her tights had holes in and her skirt needed ironing. If she were going to go through with the interview, she thought, she would have to play the part properly. She had always enjoyed drama at school. She drove to Burnside. The road was empty and the afternoon was very still. The trees were almost bare and the detail of the branches was sharp against the clear sky. There were threads of mist in the valley near the stream. She drove through the massive privet hedges which shielded the house from the road and parked on the gravel. She had never seen beyond the hedge before and was surprised by the ugliness of the house.

The interview was more formal than Patty had expected. She knew that Mrs Mount needed staff quickly and had thought there would be a pleasant chat about Patty's attitude to old people. Instead she was asked to wait in a hall, decorated with brown wallpaper and where there was no natural light, until Mrs Mount was ready to see her. As she waited she grew nervous as if she really wanted employment and began to rehearse what she would say. She looked into the residents' lounge, where an assistant was lifting a fat old man into a wheelchair, and wondered if she would have the patience for the work. Eventually she was shown into Mrs Mount's room.

Angela's mother sat behind a desk. She was wearing a blue blouse with a large bow and Patty thought she had chosen it to look like Mrs Thatcher. Her lacquered hair was shiny and hard as a helmet.

'Sit down, Mrs Atkins,' she said, and smiled.

Patty sat on a small wooden chair. Behind her a budgerigar began to mutter to itself. She wondered what she was doing there. How could it help to find out who had killed Medburn and Paul Wilcox?

'So you'd like to work at Burnside?' Mrs Mount asked.

'Yes,' Patty said. She grinned and tried to look enthusiastic.

'Do you live locally?' She spoke slowly, as if to a backward child.

'Yes,' Patty said. 'On the new estate. Quite close to your daughter.' The woman's patronizing attitude was starting to annoy her.

Mrs Mount looked at her sharply.

'Do you know Angela?' she asked.

'Oh yes,' Patty said. 'She suggested that I should apply for the job. She said she thought I would fit in here.'

'Oh?' Mrs Mount said, her face still rigid with the habitual smile. 'I wonder what she meant by that.'

'I think she meant that I would have the flexibility to do what was needed.'

Mrs Mount was becoming less sure of herself. She felt there was some significance behind Patty's words she had failed to understand, that she might even be the object of a veiled sarcasm. She changed the subject.

'Have you any nursing qualifications?' she asked. 'Of course we prefer our staff to be qualified.'

'No,' Patty said. 'I worked in an office before I had the children.'

'Any experience of nursing the elderly?'

'Not exactly,' Patty said. 'I looked after my mother. She was very ill but she was only fifty-eight when she died. I helped the district nurse when she came to treat her.'

'Which nurse was that?' Mrs Mount seemed to regret the question as soon as it was asked.

'Mrs Medburn,' Patty said. 'I understand that she used to work here. Before she died.'

'Did she tell you that?'

'Oh yes,' Patty said. 'She told me all about Burnside.'

The words were simple but they triggered a dramatic response in Mrs Mount. Her smile disappeared. She stared at Patty, her lipstick-red mouth slightly open, her long, sharp canine teeth protruding to the lower lip. Patty was suddenly frightened and thought it had been a mistake to have come.

'Did Mrs Medburn explain our routine to you?' The smile returned and Patty thought how foolish she had been to be scared. She was determined to achieve something from the visit to Burnside, something to take back to Ramsay.

'She told me that some of the old people took a drug at night to help them sleep,' she said. 'It was called Heminevrin.'

There was a vicious silence. There was no attempt now to pretend that this was an interview for a job.

'What are you doing here?' Mrs Mount hissed. She leaned across the desk towards Patty. 'Why are you snooping? Who are you?'

'I want to know,' Patty said, 'about the Heminevrin.'

'What do you mean?'

'Did you notice, for example, that any was missing? Did you finish the bottle sooner than you would have expected? Who collected the prescription for you?'

'Get out,' Mrs Mount said. Her face was drained of all colour so her scarlet lips seemed unnaturally bright and glossy. Patty was reminded suddenly of a vampire in a horror film and she wanted to giggle. The situation had turned into a farce.

'I'm sorry,' she said. 'I didn't mean to upset you. I should have explained before why I'm here.'

But Mrs Mount was beyond explanation. 'I won't talk to you,' she said. 'I don't care who you've been speaking to. What goes on here is none of your business. Now get out.'

She calmed herself quite suddenly and stood upright behind her desk. It was as if nothing unusual had happened. She was in charge again and the smile had returned.

'I shouldn't make any accusations you can't substantiate,' she said. 'There's been quite enough unpleasantness in Heppleburn already, don't you think, with two murders and a suicide?' She shouted to a woman waiting in the shadowy hall: 'Margaret dear, show Mrs Atkins out. I don't think she comes up to the standards we require of our staff.'

In the car Patty sat for a few moments before driving away. She was shaking with relieved tension but satisfied with her achievement. Mrs Mount was terrified. She must know something about Angela and was obviously trying to protect her. Perhaps a quantity of the drug had disappeared after her daughter had been to visit. Perhaps Angela had confessed to the murder of Medburn. How pleased Ramsay would be with the information! Patty was convinced that Angela was the murderer. She had only to prove it.

As she drove back into the village she saw that the mist in the valley had thickened and when she arrived, breathless, in the playground to collect the children, it was almost dark.

Chapter Eleven

The fog rose in the valley like a tide. At the foot of the school wall it was as if it had reached high water, because above the school and the church the sky was clear and the stars were shining. In the valley it was grey, mixed with coal dust and smoke, and it smelled of sulphur. The cars moved slowly through the village and the orange street lamps gave off no light. Ramsay parked outside the Northumberland Arms and stood for a moment in the doorway of the pub, his back to the warmth and brightness. He had very little time. There had been calls from the press that he should be replaced on the case. He was only at work now because his superior was indecisive and weak, but Ramsay knew that soon he would be forced into action. He must have a successful result by then. He had never been a sociable policeman. The practical jokes with which his colleagues had relieved the stress of their work had never amused him. He had never been particularly liked. Now he knew they were watching his discomfort with the same childish glee as they had used to plan their infantile pranks.

Ramsay decided to walk to Matthew Carpenter's flat. As he walked away from the Northumberland Arms he was surprised to see Jack Robson coming in the opposite direction, carrying a small suitcase. He supposed Patty had persuaded him to stay with her. He would have stopped to talk to him, but Jack turned quickly into the public house. Ramsay walked on. The more he thought about Medburn's murder, the more he was convinced that Carpenter was the culprit. He had motive – he had been victimized by Medburn and threatened with dismissal. He had opportunity – he had a key to the school and could have bought the bandages for the noose from some busy chemist in the town days before.

It was true that the pharmacist who owned the flat swore that no Heminevrin was missing from his shop and was indignant at the suggestion that Matthew might have stolen it. His drug cabinet was always locked, he said, and Matthew had no key to that. Yet it seemed too much of a coincidence to Ramsay. Carpenter's demeanour on the night of the murder pointed to some crisis. He had been drunk, unbalanced, obviously upset by something, and he had left the party early. Perhaps murder was an overreaction to Medburn's unfairness, but he was young, alone, an outsider from the south. All that Ramsay needed was a confession.

The shop was in a terrace which faced the Morpeth road. Matthew's flat was approached from the back by a flagged footpath which led to another similar row of houses. After leaving the Northumberland Arms Ramsay saw no one. The fog and two murders had kept people at home.

When Matthew opened the door he seemed flustered and nervous as if he had been startled from sleep. There was a narrow staircase which led over the shop to the flat. Ramsay went up first and walked into the living room. Matthew followed him and stood awkwardly in the middle. It was a very small flat. Through an open door Ramsay could see the kitchen and a mound of plates on the draining board. The room was furnished with shabby, elderly pieces donated perhaps by aunts or grandparents who wanted to contribute to his first home. It was warm, heated by an old-fashioned gas fire, which hissed and provided a comforting background for their words. A tabby kitten sat on the chair nearest to the fire. Matthew lifted it off carefully and held it. Like a child with a teddy bear, Ramsay thought derisively. Matthew moved away to offer the policeman the seat.

'Would you like some tea?' he asked, eager to please. 'I was just going to make some.' His head was bent over the kitten and he did not look at Ramsay.

'No,' Ramsay said briskly. 'I'm too busy to drink tea.' He had been drinking tea that afternoon, talking to his team in Otterbridge police station, but he wanted to intimidate Carpenter and show that he meant business. He was hoping that the teacher would lose his nerve. It had become clear to him that Carpenter dreaded the questions, hated the interviews. Ramsay thought that with sufficient gentle pressure he would be persuaded to confess.

'Just a few more questions,' Ramsay said easily. Matthew sat on the floor on the other side of the fire, his legs stretched before him, the kitten on his knee. Ramsay was disconcerted by the informality of the seating arrangement. He could only see the man's forehead and his mop of curly hair. By choosing to sit on the floor Matthew seemed casual and relaxed. It indicated a greater confidence than Ramsay thought Carpenter possessed.

'Do you own a car?' he asked, though he knew the answer already.

'No,' Matthew said. 'I can't afford one yet. I'm saving up.'

'But do you drive?'

'Yes. I passed my test when I was eighteen before I went to college. It was a birthday present from my parents.'

'Do you have access to a car?'

'Only my mother's when I go home.'

'Where does she live?'

'Derbyshire.'

So, Ramsay thought, if Carpenter had murdered Wilcox he had followed him on foot or borrowed a car, or stolen one. He had decided to concentrate tonight on the Wilcox murder. It was more recent, less fraught with complication than that of Medburn, and the attempt to prove that Carpenter had stolen Heminevrin was getting nowhere. If he could find evidence that the teacher had been near to the old mill that day he would at least have grounds for bringing him in for interview. All day his men had been asking questions at the scattered farms and cottages along the lane from the old mill to the coast, but there had been no result.

'What were you doing on Sunday?' Ramsay asked, as if it were a casual question, of no real importance. He had asked the question before and Matthew seemed irritated by it.

'I've already told you. I was here.'

'You didn't go out at all?'

Perhaps there was a slight hesitation, but without seeing Carpenter's face it was hard to tell. 'No,' Carpenter said. 'Not at all.'

'I remember now,' Ramsay said. 'You spent the day with Miss Hunt.' What was he doing with her? Ramsay thought. He's young. Hasn't he got a girlfriend? Someone he can talk to? Or perhaps he confided in the schoolmistress? He seemed to need someone to depend on.

'Miss Hunt came to lunch,' Matthew said defensively. 'She's been very kind to me since I started at the school. I would never have survived there without her. She lives on her own. I thought it would be a kind thing to do.'

He's talking too much, Ramsay thought.

'What time did she arrive?' Wilcox had been murdered soon after mid-day. Matthew could have killed him and still be back for lunch-time.

Matthew shrugged and for the first time in the interview he looked directly at the policeman. He was slightly flushed. 'I'm not sure. Late morning. I told her to come for coffee. It must have been about eleven thirty.'

'And what time did she leave?'

'Three thirty. We both had work to prepare for the next day.'

If Matthew had company for the whole of that time he could not possibly have been the murderer. Ramsay was still not convinced but changed the direction of the questions.

'Have you got any walking boots?'

'Yes.' Matthew seemed shocked. 'Why?'

'There were prints in the mud near Paul Wilcox's body. We want to compare them with the boots belonging to everyone involved in this case.'

'But I'm not involved!' Matthew said, his control suddenly slipping. 'I've told you that.'

'Its a routine matter,' Ramsay said. 'They'll have to go for forensic tests. Police work's all routine.' And bluff, he thought. What prints they'd found near the body had been churned by tractor tyres and covered by Patty Atkins's big feet. Still he had achieved his objective. The teacher seemed suitably shaken.

'I'll fetch them,' he said. He went out through the kitchen door and returned with a pair of brown boots.

Ramsay held them together by the open ends and looked at the soles.

'They're remarkably clean for boots,' he said. 'Cleaned them recently, have you?'

Matthew shook his head. 'I haven't used them since I moved here.'

There was a pause. Matthew was obviously hoping the policeman would leave, but Ramsay made no move.

'I'll have to check with Miss Hunt that the times you gave me for Sunday are correct,' he said. 'You do realize that?'

'Of course,' Matthew said. 'Of course.'

As Ramsay drove north out of Heppleburn the fog cleared, except for swirls of mist which blew from the hedge over the road. He decided that there was something peculiar about the lunch-time meeting of Irene Hunt and Matthew Carpenter. She had told him about it in previous questions but had been reticent about the details. His conviction that Matthew was a murderer made that suspicious. He turned off the main road towards the coast and the fog was thicker as he approached the sea, so he had to concerntrate on driving. The light in the farmhouse window appeared suddenly out of the fog before he realized he had reached the end of the lane. He parked by the bungalow.

Miss Hunt came quickly to the door. She must have heard the car in the lane.

'Inspector Ramsay?' she said. She sounded frightened. 'Has anything happened?'

'No,' he said. 'I just want to ask a few more questions.'

'Oh. Yes, of course. Come in.' She was courteous and distant as always. Her southern accent sounded dated, trapped in the time when she had first come north. It was untainted by Geordie. She was like a Victorian lady explorer determined to maintain standards even in the jungle.

There was a fire in the room that looked over the sea. The curtains were drawn and there was a soft, low light. The walls were covered with her watercolours.

'Would you like a drink?' she said. 'Sherry?'

'That would be very pleasant.' It was a peaceful room. Away from the school he found her less frightening. He thought she might help him.

'I'd like to confirm your movements for Sunday, Miss Hunt.' He tried to sound formal and businesslike. 'I understand you had lunch with Mr Carpenter.'

'Yes,' she said. She handed him a glass and sat on the other side of the fire. She seemed not to realize how important it was to him. 'It was very pleasant. How encouraging it is to find that men are so much more practical than they were in my youth! It was a splendid meal.'

'What time did you arrive at his home?' Ramsay asked, and held his breath as she paused to think.

'Between quarter past and half past eleven,' she said at last and he could have wept with disappointment.

'And what time did you leave?'

'Mid-afternoon. At about half past three. Matthew offered me tea but I felt I'd imposed long enough.'

'You didn't leave the house during that time?'

'No,' she said. 'We contemplated taking a walk but the weather was very disappointing. We stayed in and had a long, leisurely lunch. As I've explained he was really a very good cook.'

'Thank you,' Ramsay said. 'I'm sorry to have disturbed you.' It occurred to him for a moment that she was lying to protect the boy, but she was like a Victorian lady and the idea was unthinkable.

Jim was reluctant to let Patty out again that evening. He sat at the supper table and looked at her over his spectacles like a fat, tousled owl. His jersey had frayed sleeves and there was an old darn at the elbow. He shouldn't go to school looking like that, she thought. Perhaps she should go through his clothes and throw some of the jumble away. Or perhaps, she thought again, he could do it himself.

'You can't go out on your own,' he said. 'I'd worry about you. And I can't come with you. There's no one else to mind the bairns.'

She was grateful that he took her seriously. He even seemed to want to be involved. Recently he seemed to have been irritated by her enthusiasms, dismissive of her interests. This concern and attention were unusual, but he had surprised her before. When she first met him he was at university. Her mam and dad had been impressed by that. She had expected him to be different from the other lads in the village, to talk about books or politics, but he spent all his spare time in the bar, and when he moved his mouth away from the glass he talked about Newcastle United. Their dates were at football matches, clubs and rock concerts. He had surprised her with his proposal of marriage after all his talk of independence and freedom and his jeers at the weddings of his friends. He had also surprised her by 'his decision to become a teacher – she had thought him too selfish – but he enjoyed it and with his own children he was patient and amusing. Now, suddenly, he seemed to understand that she was facing some sort of crisis. She had never realized that he was so perceptive.

'I need to speak to Hannah Wilcox,' she said. 'She's all alone in that great house. She needs the company.'

'Will Ramsay be there?'

She looked at him sharply. 'No,' she said. 'No, of course not. Why should he be?' He's jealous, she thought, and was surprised again.

'I don't know,' Jim said unhappily. 'I thought he might have asked to meet you again. He seems to have confidence in you.'

'He took me to the pub to ask some questions about Angela Brayshaw,' she cried. 'There was no more to it than that.'

'I know.' He was trying so hard to be understanding that he was pulling strange, strained faces, as the children did when they were constipated. She smiled and kissed him.

'People are talking,' he said, 'about you and Ramsay.'

'Do you mind?'

Before he could answer the doorbell rang and there was Ramsay, his face gaunt and grooved through lack of sleep. Patty never found out if Jim believed that he was there by chance.

'I'm sorry to disturb you,' the inspector said. 'I was wondering if there was a chance of some coffee.'

'I was just on my way out,' Patty said, angry because he had put her in such an awkward position, 'to visit Hannah Wilcox.' Then because she wanted to boast about her initiative in applying for the job at Burnside: 'I suppose it can wait until the morning, Jim wasn't happy about me going out anyway.'

So Ramsay sat in the most comfortable chair in the room, with Jim glowering at him from the corner where he was marking a pile of dog-eared exercise books and Patty sitting on the floor in front of the fire.

The interviews with Matthew Carpenter and Irene Hunt had left Ramsay drained and disappointed. The hope that he would persuade Matthew to confess to the murders had left him, and he had no energy to start again. It was only as Patty told him the story of the visit to Burnside, with humour and much irrelevant detail, that his interest returned. He began to relax, to believe again that he might succeed before the pressure to remove him from the case grew too great for his superiors to resist. When he left the house it was very late and he felt refreshed as if he had slept for a long time.

Angela had enjoyed an afternoon's window shopping in Newcastle. She had wandered through Eldon Square and down Northumberland Street and knew that the things she saw in the shop windows were within her grasp. There was no need to buy. There was pleasure enough in looking and planning and knowing the pressure of debt had been removed. Some of the stores had started to decorate the windows for Christmas and the streets were busy with well-organized women doing Christmas shopping. This year will be different, she thought. There'll be no skimping this year, and she imagined the presents she would buy for Claire. She could afford the best food, the most expensive decorations. The day would be perfect, as the articles in the women's magazines she read said it could be. David would be sorry he had ever left her.

She left before the shops shut. There was no hurry because Claire was going to a friend's for tea, but Angela thought it was time to face her mother. She had parked on the quayside and sat in the car, watching the lights come on over the Tyne Bridge, thinking what she would say. The London train moved slowly across the river towards the station. She had already told her mother that she would not be working at Burnside because Medburn had left her enough money to repay the debt. She knew that she would receive a great deal. Beside his savings there was a house in Tynemouth he had bought years before in preparation for his retirement. But she had given her mother no details. She had not explained why Medburn had left her the money. Everyone else in Heppleburn knew and her mother would have heard the gossip by now. It was time to put her point of view. She drove over the cobbles through the darkening streets along the quay, past the multi-coloured brickwork of the Byker wall and along the coast towards Heppleburn.

Angela had guessed her mother might be angry about the rumours circulating in the village about herself and Medburn, but she had never seen the woman in such a state. For as long as Angela could remember, Mrs Mount had been composed and stately. There had been a few seemly tears at her husband's funeral, the occasional outburst or irritation when one of the staff at Burnside had not followed her instructions precisely, but throughout these her control had remained intact. Now she was almost unrecognizable. She did not shout or cry, but the impression of strength and power had gone. She was vulnerable, small, weak. The whole place seemed to be in disorder. Usually tea had been served and cleared away by five o'clock, but when Angela arrived the residents were still at the table. There were remnants of the meal on plates in front of them sandwich crusts, half-eaten pieces of scone, the plain biscuits which no one had chosen – like the debris after a children's tea party.

An old man was shouting that he needed the toilet and the staff were too harassed to go to his assistance. Angela took his arm and helped him. Surprisingly, because she knew now that this was done voluntarily, she felt no resentment at being required to help. When he was back in his chair she went to find her mother.

Mrs Mount was in her room, sitting behind her desk, and she looked tired. Angela had never seen her anything but fresh, brisk and efficient. The exhaustion made her seem more human and Angela realized suddenly how much she must have been hurt by her daughter's refusal to work with her.

'You must have had a busy day,' Angela said.

Mrs Mount looked up.

'What are you doing here?' she said. 'Haven't you caused trouble enough?'

'I'm sorry,' Angela said. 'I know there'll be gossip. But it'll soon be over and they'll find something else to stick their nebby noses in.'

'I've worked hard for this place,' Mrs Mount said. 'You think it was easy.'

'No,' Angela said. 'I never thought that.' But it *had* seemed easy for Mrs Mount who swept through the place with her smile and her dignity, seeming not to notice the loneliness, humiliation, or smell of her residents.

'I knew what I wanted,' Mrs Mount continued, 'and I did what I had to do to get it.' She looked at her daughter. 'Just like you and Medburn.' It was the only time the man was mentioned throughout the conversation.

'Why don't you sell the place and retire?' Angela asked. 'You'd get a good price for it.' But she could not imagine her mother powerless, with only herself to organize, having to cook her own meals and make her own bed. She brought me up to be spoiled and waited on too, Angela thought. For the whole of my childhood I was told I was special. Well, I am special now. The sudden insight chilled her.

'How can I retire until I know what's going to happen?' The woman turned on her in anger.

'What do you mean?'

'There was a woman here this afternoon. She'd pretended to

come about a job as care assistant, but she was here asking questions. She said you'd sent her.'

'What was her name?'

'Atkins.'

Angela was shocked. She supposed she should have expected it, but she had never thought Patty would have the application to see the thing through.

'She's Jack Robson's daughter,' she said. 'You know, he's the old man who always claimed that Kitty Medburn was innocent of the murder. She was helping him find out about it. I never sent her here.'

'She knew too much,' Mrs Mount said. 'She was asking about the Heminevrin. What if Kitty Medburn talked to Robson before she died?' She looked with desperation at her daughter. 'You'll have to do something about them. I can't have either of them talking to the police.'

Throughout the day Jack Robson had begun to emerge from the cocoon of numb sadness which had protected him from his grief. The exhaustion and apathy which had kept him in his armchair for days disappeared suddenly, as if he had recovered from a serious illness. He cooked and ate a large meal and enjoyed it, tasting every mouthful.

The memory of Kitty in the prison and the school house was sharp and painful, but he was no longer overwhelmed by it. Like the image of Kitty as a girl, skipping in the school playground, he saw the recent past as a piece of fiction, read and passionately reacted to, but in the end unreal. His infatuation for her seemed like an illness too, a fever. He wondered how it could ever have happened. All that was left was a sense of guilt and responsibility, and Jack had too strong an instinct for survival, too little imagination to be devastated by that. He was more at home with action and as he took control of his life again, he wondered what he should do.

What would Joan say? he thought and that too was an indication that things were returning to normal, because since his wife's death he had asked the question many times. He could almost hear her speaking: 'Get off your backside, Jack Robson! It's no good moping around the house. You've work to do.'

What work? he thought. Hadn't he caused enough damage with his meddling? Yet he longed for the sense of purpose which the original investigation had given him. The excitement, the questions, the exhilaration of discovery were addictive. He wanted to see a result. He wanted to go to Ramsay and see the policeman's face when he told him the name of the murderer. Although that was still a long way off Jack felt that he might know who had killed Medburn. Almost unconsciously, as he sat in his stupor of mourning, he had been worrying at the problem of the headmaster's death and had developed a theory so unlikely, so bizarre, that it seemed like a feverish nightmare. Yet it answered all the questions. He wondered now what he should do to prove it, and his wife's words came to him again: 'Jack Robson. Get off your backside!'

On an impulse he got out of his chair and made a telephone call to the coach station in Newcastle. He found out that there was an evening coach to the south. He returned to his chair and thought for a few minutes.

There was the same feeling of health and vitality that had come to him earlier. His head was full of ideas and plans. He went upstairs and packed the small suitcase he had bought for Joan to take to hospital when she was first ill. He was ready. Only then did it occur to him that his daughter might be worried if he suddenly disappeared. He was too excited to tell her. She would think he was mad to rush off into the night with nowhere to stay, and would stop him going. He felt he was coming out of a period of insanity but it would be hard to explain that to her. In the end he wrote to Patty. His note said very little. He needed time to think, he said. He would go away for a few days. She wasn't to worry. He did not tell her his destination. Perhaps he wanted to create a mystery of his disappearance, to make himself important. He gave his neighbour's son a pound coin to deliver the letter the next morning on his way to school.

He looked at his watch. It was too early yet to get a taxi into

Newcastle but he wanted to be out of the house. Now he had decided on action he could sit for no longer. In the street he saw Ramsay hurrying through the fog, and felt smug and triumphant because he was sure the policeman was on the wrong track altogether. In the Northumberland Arms he drank a pint of beer, and it felt like a celebration.

Chapter Twelve

The news of Jack's disappearance spread round the village and as time went on the rumours grew wilder and more unlikely. He had been seen by the customers of the Northumberland Arms to get into a taxi. Some claimed to have heard the destination. They had noted his suitcase and before Patty received his letter the following day the gossip had already started. He'd had to get away, some said, because he was so upset by Kitty's death, but the men in the Northumberland Arms discounted that, he hadn't looked upset to them. He was like his old self. He'd had a bit of a joke and he'd bought a round. No one listened to them for long. Rumour was more exciting than reality. Women in the bus queue, shopping bags at their feet, discussed it. One suggested that he intended to commit suicide too. Perhaps he could not face life without Kitty. The other women were enchanted. The idea brought romance to the grey, November day. It was like being at the pictures.

By the time Patty had dropped the children at school the gossip was more vicious. There was speculation that he was running away from the police. He had killed Paul Wilcox, people said, to prove Kitty's innocence. They had been having an affair for years, since before Joan's death. Kitty had killed Medburn to set herself free, then Jack had murdered Wilcox to throw suspicion elsewhere. Now he had run away. Patty heard the gossip in the schoolyard and the playground and wherever she went she felt their curiosity and sympathy. She was angry and worried, and wondered what on earth her father was doing.

Ramsay learned of Jack's disappearance in the school. The teachers were grumbling because the caretaker had not arrived and no one else knew how to work the boiler. The cleaner, whose husband had been in the Northumberland Arms the night before, told of his suitcase and the taxi which had come to take him to Newcastle.

'I saw him with his suitcase,' Ramsay said casually. 'I thought he was going to stay at his daughter's.' Poor old bugger, he thought. I don't blame him for wanting to get away.

He was back at the school, asking questions with a renewed energy, a nervous frenzy. He had been given to the end of the week to get a result. Then he would be moved to what his boss called a 'less sensitive assignment'. Patty's confidence in him had provided a new determination to prove them all wrong. He stayed around the school through a kind of superstition, as if the answer to the case was in the stone walls if only he knew the magic to release it. By mid-morning he realized he was being foolish and knew he was in the way. He left the school and went out into the damp and gloomy village.

Patty saw Ramsay next at six o'clock that evening. Jim had come home from work and the children were watching television. She was in the kitchen peeling potatoes and it was Jim who opened the door to him.

'Yes?' she heard her husband say. 'What do you want?'

'Can I speak to Patty?'

'Aye. I suppose you'd better come in.'

The three of them stood in the small kitchen and Jim looked at the policeman with obvious hostility.

'Have you seen your father?' Ramsay asked.

'No,' she said. 'You know as well as I do. You'll have heard all the gossip. He's gone away for a few days.'

'No,' Ramsay said. 'He phoned me up this afternoon. It was a peculiar phone call. I wasn't sure if he was quite sober. He said he knew who had killed Medburn and Wilcox and that he'd meet me at his house to tell me all about it as soon as he got back. He was expecting to be here by five. I've been hanging around for him.'

'He hasn't been in touch with me today.' She was offended. Why hadn't her father consulted her before disappearing? She had thought they were partners. 'Where was he phoning from?'

'He didn't say. He didn't say much. He was in a call box and his money had run out. Or perhaps he didn't want to tell me any more. It was somewhere noisy. A bus station probably. There was the sound of engines and a crackly public address system.' He looked at Patty. 'You've no idea where he might be?'

'No,' she said. 'I don't think I understand him at all any more.'

'He's no fool,' Jim said. 'Not Jack. He can look after himself.'

'I'll talk to the taxi driver who picked him up yesterday evening,' Ramsay said, 'We'll see if we can find out where he's been.' He found it a relief to have something concrete to do. He touched Patty on the shoulder. 'Don't worry!' he said. 'We'll find him and get him back.'

Jack had arrived later than he had expected. There had been traffic jams on the A1, and the town was further south than he had realized. It was midnight when he climbed out of the coach, stiff and bleary-eyed. He had slept on and off. The place was strange to him and he felt he did not have sufficient courage to leave the bus station and go out into the town to find somewhere to stay. It was surely too late for that and bus stations were the same everywhere, so he felt safe where he was. The waiting room had not been locked. He found a chair there and, surrounded by overflowing rubbish bins and clutching the handle of his suitcase, he slept.

Early in the morning he was woken by cleaners and the noise of the first buses. He washed and shaved in the public lavatory and went out into the town. In a cobbled market square, stalls were being erected. He felt light-hearted and brave like a soldier in his first action. He might have been in a foreign country with the strange accents all around him, the different beer advertised on the hoardings, the unfamiliar people. He had never seen so many Asian people and the glittering saris and the exotic fruit and vegetables on the market stalls fascinated him. There were students carrying books and files and men in suits on their way to the office. He felt he had led a completely sheltered life. There had been the grime of the pit and the grey houses of Heppleburn, and he had missed out on all this colour. He understood why his elder daughter never came home.

He found an Italian café in a side street where a group of workmen were eating breakfast. They were speaking in Italian, very loudly, shouting jokes to the proprietors over the sound of the espresso machine and the jukebox. He was hungry and ate a fried breakfast and a pile of toast. He could have stayed there all morning, watching the customers, enjoying the warmth and the noise.

At nine o'clock he went into an estate agent's office and asked if they had a map of the town. He was afraid they would not give him one unless they thought he was a serious purchaser, so he came out with an armful of property details too. He put the glossy brochures of alarmingly expensive houses into a bin and sat on a bench in a covered precinct to read the map.

Ashton Road was a pleasant, red-brick terrace opposite the park. There were trees in the gardens, with russet-coloured leaves, and the sun caught the latticed window panes. They were unpretentious houses, ordinary, but in his mood of discovery and new experience he thought they were beautiful. The warm brick and the tall chimneys enchanted him. He walked down the pavement, his head turned towards them like a tourist walking through London for the first time.

The house he wanted was at the end of the terrace, on a corner. There were black wrought-iron gates into a small garden, where one late rose was still in bloom. What must I look like, he thought, standing here? Like those chaps on the dole who go round selling dusters at the door. What will she think?

He rang the bell and a dog barked. A woman opened the door to him. She was tall and slender, with a nervous, worried face. He knew immediately that he had come to the right place.

'Mrs Carpenter?' he said. 'I wonder if I could speak to you. It's about your son.' She stood aside to let him in.

On the way home the bus stopped at York and he phoned Ramsay. He was tired by then and the noise all around him prevented him from thinking or speaking clearly. It took a long time to get put through to him. He realized he must sound confused and elated to the policeman, but no longer cared. Soon he would share the responsibility of knowledge and it would all be over. When he returned to the bus it was full and noisy and he had no chance to sleep. It was late afternoon when they arrived at Newcastle. He was relieved to be almost home. He thought he would catch a bus to Heppleburn – he had spent too much already on this escapade and a taxi would be an extravagance – but when he got out at the Haymarket Miss Hunt was there in her red Metro.

'Mr Robson,' she said. 'What a coincidence! Come in and I'll give you a lift.'

He hesitated for a moment, but he was tired and not thinking clearly. Besides, it was one way of finding out if he were right. In his mood of exhilaration he thought he was invincible. It was only when he had lifted his suitcase on to the back seat and had sat comfortably on the passenger seat that he realized a shotgun was resting on her knee, the barrel pointing towards him. It was partly hidden by her long black cape.

'I knew when to meet you,' she said. 'I received a telephone call at the school this morning. It was from my daughter.' The mask of politeness slipped and her voice changed. 'The policeman was in the office when I took the phone call. I found that rather amusing.' She began to laugh.

She drove out of the city and took the road north, so he knew she was taking him to her bungalow, not to Heppleburn. In his absence the fog had thickened and the police had lit burning braziers to mark the roundabouts. The cars crawled from one cat's eye to the next and he had no idea where he was.

'Where did you get the gun?' he asked. The question had been troubling him during the drive through Newcastle. Her silence was unnerving him too and he wanted to get her to speak to him.

'From my elderly neighbour,' Irene Hunt said. 'She keeps it to protect herself from imagined intruders. She's so confused that she won't notice that it's gone. I took the Heminevrin from her too.

The doctor prescribed it for her months ago, but she'd forgotten all about it and there was nearly a bottle left.'

He realized that they must be in Nellington. The illuminated sign of the pub lurched crazily out of the fog above them. She turned off the main road towards the sea, though he did not see the junction or the signpost. It was so black that he did not know how she kept to the road.

'When did you find out that Matthew was your grandson?' he asked.

She smiled fondly but her voice was firm. 'No more questions,' she said. 'Not until we get home. I don't want to put the car in the ditch. You might run away. But don't be anxious. I'll satisfy your curiosity before I kill you.'

She had left the light on in the bungalow porch, so he knew they had arrived. There was no light in the farmhouse, though somewhere in the darkness he could hear the dogs howling as if they had been chained for the night.

'It's no good shouting,' Irene Hunt said. 'The old lady's deaf and even if she were to hear you she'd take no notice.' She got out of the car and locked the door meticulously behind her. 'Come on,' she said, suddenly irritated like a child denied a treat. 'Come inside. I want to tell you all about it.'

Jack followed her. He left his suitcase inside the car and thought it unlikely that he would need it now. Inside, she drew all the curtains and put a light to the fire. It caught immediately and the flames were reflected on the walls of the room and her eager face.

'Sit down,' she said, as if he were some friend who had called in without invitation. 'You must be tired.'

'It never occurred to me,' he said, 'that Mrs Carpenter might phone you.'

'We're very close,' she said proudly.

'Yet she never told Matthew about you.'

'That was her husband's fault,' she said. 'When the children were young they were close to her adoptive parents. He'd never let her tell them the truth. He said it would confuse them. When he left her she didn't want to admit that she'd lied. She did persuade

Matthew to apply for the job at Heppleburn. That was kind. As it turned out it was just as well Matthew never knew I was his grandmother. It was difficult enough for him at Heppleburn without Medburn knowing he was a relative of mine.'

Jack sat in a large, comfortable armchair. He felt as if he were slipping into sleep. Miss Hunt held the gun lightly across her lap and he was almost too tired to care if she used it or not. But he did want to know what had happened and it occurred to him that the longer he could persuade her to keep talking, the more chance there was that he would survive.

'Why did you kill Medburn?' he asked.

'Because of Matthew, of course,' she said fiercely. 'The headmaster had been tormenting me for years, but that was different. I love Matthew. He's the only relative I've had to care for. He had to be protected.'

Her voice was high-pitched and wild and he wondered why none of them had realized before how desperate she was. He supposed they were so used to her that they took her for granted. They did not look behind the formal, authoritarian exterior. And she was convinced that her action was justified. She had no cause to show fear or remorse.

'You killed Medburn because he was going to sack Matthew?' She nodded.

'He told me on the day of the Harvest Festival,' she said. 'Do you remember? It was the day of the Parents' Association committee meeting when your daughter suggested that we had the Hallowe'en party. I thought: if only I were a witch. I'd shape a spell and make him disappear for ever. Then I decided I'd kill him anyway. It wasn't as if he was worth anything. He had no intrinsic value. He was an ugly little man. I couldn't see anything wrong in it.'

She was rambling and Jack looked at the gun, wondering whether she might forget it and allow it to slip from her knee to the floor.

'I enjoyed getting the details right,' she said. 'I told you, didn't I, that I had ambitions to be a theatre designer until my parents sent me north in disgrace? I designed it like a stage act. Anne's father was an actor . . .' She stopped, lost in thought, then continued.

'It took me longer than I expected to carry Medburn to the small playground. He was heavier than he looked.' She seemed lost in memory and the gun began to slide between her knees towards the floor, but she caught it and held it firmly. She leaned forward and talked earnestly. 'I had to plan it all,' she said, 'in every detail. It wasn't easy, you know.'

She looked up at him as if she expected approval.

'I knew about the Heminevrin,' she went on, 'because the old lady's daughter complained to me once that she couldn't get her to take it. "The doctor says it'll stop her wandering around at night," she said, "but she just spits it out because it tastes so bad. You'd think they could put something in it to make it taste better." I didn't think that would matter with Medburn because everyone knew he had no sense of taste, but even he noticed it. "This coffee isn't up to your normal standard, Miss Hunt," he said, being as pompous as ever, but he drank it all the same.'

'You must have phoned him,' Jack said, determined to maintain the conversation. 'I suppose you asked him to come back to school. How did you manage that?'

'I said I had a message from Angela Brayshaw,' she said. 'He thought he'd kept that affair secret, but everyone could tell how infatuated he was with her. He came rushing round to school like a little boy in love. I had the coffee ready, with the drug in his mug. I told him that Angela had arranged to come back to school early, so they could have some time together before the party started. He looked so pleased with himself, so smug. I pretended to leave and sat in my classroom to wait. When I went back to the hall a quarter of an hour later he was unconscious. I strangled him, then dragged him into the small playground and strung him up on the netball hoop. I had the noose ready. I was pleased with the result. He looked very ... ? dramatic hanging there. It was most appropriate for Hallowe'en. All the time I was working I was conscious that someone might come and surprise me.' She stopped and looked directly at him. 'It was exciting,' she said. 'I have never been so excited in my life. I wanted to humiliate him as he had humiliated me.'

'You were clever,' Jack said. 'I would have said that you were as surprised as the rest of us when I found his body.'

'Yes,' she said. 'I would never have thought myself capable of it. I was pleased with myself. My boyfriend would have been proud of me.'

'It must have been a bit of a shock when I turned up to talk to you,' Jack said. He felt he was entitled to be proud of himself too.

'It was,' she said. 'I didn't think anyone would find out about Anne, but I still thought I was safe . . .'

She stood up suddenly, in a jerk, as if she had heard a noise outside, and walked to the window. She peered through the curtains then returned to her chair.

'Why did you kill Paul Wilcox then?' he asked. He took a cigarette from his pocket and lit it. It seemed unimportant now that he might offend her. 'If you thought you were safe.'

She obviously disliked the implied criticism.

'Perhaps I was too clever when I followed you to the school house on the night of the bonfire,' she admitted. 'I felt helpless. I didn't know how far you'd got with your investigation. I hoped to frighten you.'

'You just made me more determined,' he said.

'Yes. I realize that.'

'Paul Wilcox was already in the school house looking for some letters he'd sent to Angela Brayshaw. He saw you, didn't he?'

'Yes,' she said. 'He was looking out of the upstairs window and he saw me in the moonlight. He seemed too frightened then to realize the implication of it, but I was worried he'd see how important it was later. I never planned to kill him. It was quite spontaneous. I was on my way to Matthew's and I saw Wilcox come out of the old mill and walk up the lane. I turned the car round and followed him. Just as I reached him it started to rain very heavily. I saw that as fate. I stopped the car beside him. "Get in," I said. "I'll give you a lift home." He didn't suspect anything. I always thought he was a fool. Then I saw him sitting there, starting to wonder. "What were you doing at the school house on the night of the bonfire?" he asked. "It was you I saw in the playground." So I had to kill him. I took my scarf and twisted it round his neck as he was turning to get out of the car. It was easy then to tip him into the ditch.'

'Wilcox had a wife and two children,' Jack said.

'He was weak and silly,' she said quickly. 'I couldn't let him get in the way.'

She's like a selfish child, he thought, determined to get her own way at any price.

'And what about me?' he cried. 'What excuse do you have for getting rid of me.'

'You were warned,' she said. 'It was your choice.' She looked quite different, hunched over the gun, her knees wide apart like one of the incontinent old ladies at Burnside. She had lost her control and dignity. Her protective passion for Matthew had destroyed her.

'Don't you think they'll realize you're the murderer if they find my body here?'

'Do you think I'm a fool?' The words exploded from her and she was so angry and unbalanced that he was afraid she would shoot him immediately. 'No one knows where you are. They think you've run away because you were depressed by Kitty's death. So depressed that you might commit suicide yourself.'

'I'd never kill myself. I'm no coward.'

'No,' she said, 'but if they find your body that's what they'll think. The bottle of Heminevrin's still nearly full. I'm stronger than you and I've got a gun. I'll take you to your home and eventually someone will find your body there. Poor Jack, they'll say, her death turned his mind. He was crazy with love.'

'*I'm* not crazy,' he said before he could stop himself.

'Are you suggesting that I am?' she spat at him. 'Because I was looking after the only person I had the opportunity of loving?'

'That's not true,' he said. 'You had plenty of opportunity, a fine young woman like you. Perhaps you were crazy even then, brooding about that man who got you in trouble.'

He had provoked her too far. She stood up and pointed the gun towards him. Suddenly there was a knock at the door. She swung round, confused and bewildered as if the noise had emptied her mind of all thought.

'Keep away!' she shouted. 'Keep away or I'll kill him.'

There was another knock. She prowled towards the window and looked out but the porch light was off and there was nothing to see. Jack sat quietly, unmoving.

'Who is it?' she shouted. 'Who's there?'

The unknown person knocked on the door again. The noise and the lack of response seemed to irritate her. She edged towards the door.

Suddenly there was the sound of breaking glass as the back door into the kitchen was broken. The room seemed full of policemen. Ramsay was there and Irene Hunt had collapsed on the floor, an old and ugly woman, her face wrinkled and running with tears.

'She must be mad,' Jack said. He felt he had to make an excuse for her. He hoped they would treat her gently.

'She would have killed you,' the policeman said. 'You'd better come home. I promised Patty I'd get you back safely.'

As they walked up the lane to where the cars had been parked out of earshot of the bungalow, Jack found that the fog was lifting in patches and he could see stars above his head.

Chapter Thirteen

Patty's small living room seemed full of people. Ramsay was there, quite at home in Jim's chair, his legs stretched out in front of the fire. Hannah Wilcox had turned up on the doorstep without warning. She had heard about Jack's disappearance, she said, and wondered if she could do anything, to help. This unexpected gesture of friendship and support pleased Patty almost more than the safe arrival of her father. She pulled Hannah in and persuaded her to stay, although she said it was a family affair and they would want to be left alone. Now Hannah sat on the floor in a corner, trying unsuccessfully to be inconspicuous, because whenever she spoke or moved she demanded attention. Jim, solid and relieved, wished the visitors would go away so life could return to normal. He drank beer and handed a can to Jack, and after some hesitation to Ramsay. Now he would never have to see the policeman again he was prepared to be friendly. The room was very hot. Patty remembered what Hannah had said about shock making you feel cold and had turned the heating on full.

'How did you find me then?' Jack asked. He was more relaxed than anyone.

'It was Inspector Ramsay,' Patty said. Jim recognized the admiration in her voice and seemed to shrink.

'It was easy enough to find out which coach you took,' Ramsay said. 'That was routine police work. Matthew Carpenter had told me that he came from there. The local police sent someone round to interview his mother. She said you'd been to see her and admitted that she'd phoned Miss Hunt. She didn't know Miss Hunt was involved with the murders, of course. She just thought you were going to make trouble for her, as Medburn had done. Then it was obvious to go to the bungalow. When we saw your suitcase in her car, we knew you must be inside.'

'She threatened to kill me,' Jack said. 'She was going to make it look like suicide.' It sounded very impressive. He thought everyone would make a fuss of him for months.

Hannah Wilcox cleared her throat to speak and they all looked at her. There was a brief silence except for the muffled sound of next door's television. 'Did she kill Paul?' she asked. 'I need to know.'

'Yes,' Ramsay said. 'Because he'd seen her at the school house.'

'But I thought she had an alibi. She was with Matthew Carpenter.'

'That was clever,' Ramsay said. 'Matthew realized he was under suspicion and he was frightened. Miss Hunt told him she was prepared to protect him and persuaded him to lie to me. "Tell them I got to your house an hour earlier than I actually did," she said. "I know you're not a murderer. I'll back up anything that you say." And in persuading him, of course, she provided an alibi for herself.'

Hannah lit a cigarette and passed the packet to Jack. 'Thank you,' she said. 'At least now I know what happened.'

'Poor Matthew,' Patty said. 'He'll be shattered. Did he have no idea that she was his grandmother?'

'No, why should he? He thought she was a kind teacher, close to retirement, who'd taken him under her wing.'

'I was convinced that Angela Brayshaw was the murderer,' Patty said. She was ashamed she had been so wrong. 'It seems ridiculous now but her mother behaved so peculiarly when I went to Burnside.'

'We've found out what all that was about,' Ramsay said. Jack felt he was being patronizing to Patty. He had been no closer to finding the truth than her after all. 'Mrs Mount was only too pleased to talk when she realized she was suspected of murder. Apparently she used to make all the residents of Burnside take Heminevrin at night, even those for whom it hadn't been prescribed. I suppose it made life easier for her, but it's against the law. Kitty Medburn found out what was going on there and she was shocked. She told Mrs Mount the home would have to change its way of operating or she'd tell the police. When you went for the interview and began asking questions about the drug, Mrs Mount thought Kitty had told Jack what she'd been up to. No wonder she overreacted.'

'I misjudged Angela,' Patty said. 'How dreadful to think someone capable of murder!' She would have to go to see Angela, she thought, and explain. 'But I never imagined it was Miss Hunt.'

'She had been twisted and bitter inside for forty years,' Jack said, 'without giving any sign of it at all. She told me Matthew was the only person she'd had a chance to love since her parents sent her away. Matthew was like her bairn and her man all together. She couldn't keep that sort of pretence!'

'What was her daughter like?'

'Dark and pretty like Miss Hunt was twenty years ago. She's unhappy too. She seemed to me to brood too much on the past.'

And isn't that just what I've been doing, he thought, pretending that I was a young man again, and could change decisions made years ago?

'How did you know that Matthew was Miss Hunt's grandson?' Ramsay asked. 'Did she say something at school?'

Jack shook his head. 'I knew Carpenter's home address,' he said, 'because occasionally he used to bring letters to school for me to post for him. Then on the night of the bonfire, just before I was hit on the head, I found a scrap of paper on Medburn's desk. It had Irene Hunt's name on it, but an address in the Midlands. Medburn must have written it when Anne Carpenter came to Heppleburn to find her mother. The address seemed familiar but I didn't realize until later where I'd seen it before.'

'You should have told me,' Ramsay said.

'Aye. Perhaps I should.'

The visitors left together – Ramsay offered to drive Hannah Wilcox home and as he helped her into the car Patty felt an ache of jealousy. She remembered the fast drive to Whitley Bay with him. That would be out of the question now. She would have to live by the old rules again. She and Jack were standing on the doorstep to see the guests off. Ramsay left Hannah in the car and returned to speak to them.

'Thank you for your help,' he said. 'I should be telling you off for interfering, but I would never have found her without your help.'

'Will we see you again?' Patty asked. She spoke quietly. She did not want Jim to hear.

'Of course. You'll be needed as witnesses at the trial. I'll be in touch.' And he waved his hand and drove away.

It was not late. She could hear the signature tune for *News at Ten* from her neighbours' television. Somewhere in the street a woman was taking a dog for its evening walk. The bairns were in bed and Jim would be wanting tea and a sandwich for his supper.

'It's as if nothing ever happened,' she said. 'Everything's just the same.'

Jack thought of Kitty, the sense of vigour and clarity she had given him, the pleasure of his trip south, the excitement of achievement. He would not be content now to be a councillor and school caretaker whose only challenge was a weekly trip to the library, tedious council meetings and a pint at the club.

'No,' he said. 'Nothing will be the same again.'

After Ramsay had dropped Hannah at the mill he sat for a moment in the car. The fog had lifted and he could see the damp trees over the road. There was an immense relief that the case was over without further violence. He had been lucky. It had been a mistake to take Kitty Medburn into custody and the repercussions from that would rumble on, he supposed. But it was a mistake any of his colleagues might have made and the decision had been supported by his superiors. It would soon be forgotten by everyone but him. He would always remember it. Now, when he should be elated with success he felt empty and a little sad. He had come to think of the people who had spent the evening in Patty's home as his friends. He would miss them.

Lightning Source UK Ltd.
Milton Keynes UK
UKOW02f0319180616

276508UK00003B/28/P